Kiss from a

The Gentleman, leading his horse by the bridle, drew
it to a standstill just outside the woods.

He lifted Shenda down with ease.

To Shenda, the handsome stranger seemed to have
a strength that came not only from his athletic body,
but also from his mind.

As her feet touched the ground, she said:

"Thank you! I will never . . . forget . . . your kindness."

The stranger said quietly:

"I think you should reward me for my labors."

He put his finger under her chin, turned her face
up to his, and kissed her. . . .

Then, before the astonished Shenda could speak
or move, the stranger had ridden away. . . .

A Camfield Novel of Love
by Barbara Cartland

---

*"Barbara Cartland's novels are all distinguished by their
intelligence, good sense, and good nature . . ."*
— **ROMANTIC TIMES**

*"Who could give better advice on how to keep your romance
going strong than the world's most famous romance novelist, Barbara Cartland?"*
— **THE STAR**

Camfield Place,
Hatfield
Hertfordshire,
England

Dearest Reader,

Camfield Novels of Love mark a very exciting era of my books with Jove. They have already published nearly two hundred of my titles since they became my first publisher in America, and now all my original paperback romances in the future will be published exclusively by them.

As you already know, Camfield Place in Hertfordshire is my home, which originally existed in 1275, but was rebuilt in 1867 by the grandfather of Beatrix Potter.

It was here in this lovely house, with the best view in the county, that she wrote *The Tale of Peter Rabbit*. Mr. McGregor's garden is exactly as she described it. The door in the wall that the fat little rabbit could not squeeze underneath and the goldfish pool where the white cat sat twitching its tail are still there.

I had Camfield Place blessed when I came here in 1950 and was so happy with my husband until he died, and now with my children and grandchildren, that I know the atmosphere is filled with love and we have all been very lucky.

It is easy here to write of love and I know you will enjoy the Camfield Novels of Love. Their plots are definitely exciting and the covers very romantic. They come to you, like all my books, with love.

Bless you,

Barbara Cartland

A NEW CAMFIELD NOVEL OF LOVE BY

BARBARA CARTLAND

Kiss From a Stranger

JOVE BOOKS, NEW YORK

KISS FROM A STRANGER

A Jove Book/published by arrangement with
the author

PRINTING HISTORY
Jove edition/March 1990

All rights reserved.
Copyright © 1990 by Barbara Cartland.
Cover art copyright © 1990 by BarCart Publications (N.A.) N.V.
This book may not be reproduced in whole or in part,
by mimeograph or any other means, without permission.
For information address: The Berkley Publishing Group,
200 Madison Avenue, New York, New York 10016.

ISBN: 0-515-10273-3

Jove Books are published by The Berkley Publishing Group,
200 Madison Avenue, New York, New York 10016.
The name "JOVE" and the "J" logo
are trademarks belonging to Jove Publications, Inc.

PRINTED IN THE UNITED STATES OF AMERICA

10 9 8 7 6 5 4 3 2 1

Author's Note

The background of this novel is accurate and mostly from *The Years of Victory* by Sir Arthur Bryant.

Bonaparte's Spies were everywhere, and he did know about "The Secret Expedition." What he did not know was where it was going.

Nelson's brilliant perception took him West following the French Fleet. It was a shot in the dark, and as he said to his Secretary:

"If they are not gone to the West Indies, I shall be blamed! To be burnt in effigy, or Westminster Abbey, is my alternative."

He was right, and the same year he won the Battle of Trafalgar, saying as he lay dying: *"Thank God I have done my duty."*

Then his spirit passed and became *"One with England and the Sea."*

chapter one

1805

WALKING through the wood, Shenda was humming a little tune to herself that she thought was the music from the trees.

It was warm for April. The leaves were already in bud, and she knew that when she got a sight of the gardens at Arrow they would be brilliant with blossom.

Nothing was more beautiful than the daffodils golden under the trees, and the crocuses, yellow and purple, peeping their heads above the ground that had been so bare in the winter.

Then there were the purple and white lilacs which came into bud a few days sooner than the syringa bushes.

The woods had a magic of their own, and there was a secret place in this one, where there was a pool which she was sure was magic.

The kingcups made the borders of it golden, and the irises were reflected in the deep silver of its surface.

Whenever Shenda felt sad or lonely, she always went to her magic pool in the wood.

There she felt that fairies were watching her from amongst the flowers, the goblins were burrowing under the trees, and undoubtedly deep in the pool itself were water nymphs.

Because she was an only child, her dreams were always full of the creatures from the other world which she felt was near her.

She had always thought herself so lucky because Knight's Wood, as it was called, ended just outside the Vicarage.

While her father was busy with his Sermons or his parishioners, who always had a grievance they wanted to tell him, she would slip away by herself into the magic of the wood.

She was alone except for her most beloved companion, who was not at the moment, as he should have been, walking to heel.

He had, in fact, scented a rabbit in the undergrowth that was just beginning to cover the ground.

He had rushed after it so swiftly that Shenda was not aware that he had left her.

Rufus had been with her ever since he had been a puppy.

He was a very small, attractive spaniel who would otherwise have been trained with the other spaniels at Arrow Castle as gun-dogs.

The old Earl, who had been ill for the last three years, could no longer go shooting, and his sons were both away fighting a Monster called Napoleon Bonaparte, who was threatening to invade England.

There was therefore no shooting in the woods, and Shenda was very glad.

She hated to think of anything being killed, least of all the birds she loved and who she believed sang to her as she walked beneath the boughs of their trees.

She would sit by the magic pool where they came to drink, listening to their singing in the trees.

In fact, she could not remember what were to her the "bad old days," when there were shooting-parties in the Autumn and the keepers said there were too many magpies, weasels, and foxes in the woods.

She loved them in the same way that she loved the little red squirrels.

They would run up onto a bough at her approach, to sit chattering at her as if they thought she had come to steal their nuts.

Then, six months earlier, the Earl of Arrow died.

While his Funeral was impressive, there were few people in the village to miss him because they had not seen him for so long.

They were also, Shenda knew, not particularly distressed when they learned that the Earl's elder son, George, had been killed several months earlier in India.

The Doctor had said that the old Earl was heart-broken at the news.

"Master George," as the servants who had served at the Castle for years called him, had been in "Foreign parts" for eight years, and the younger people could not even remember what he had looked like.

This meant that his brother had come into the title, but there again, "Master Durwin" had disappeared at an early age into the Navy.

Although those who followed the news queried whether he was part of the Fleet which was defying Bonaparte by stopping the French ships from leaving their ports, nobody really knew for certain.

There had, however, been stories lately about Captain Durwin Bow.

With no-one at the Castle, the people in the village came to the Vicarage with their complaints and grievances because there was no-one to listen to them at the Castle.

The Estate Manager, who should have heard their querulous voices saying that the roof leaked, the pump did not work, or the windows were falling off their hinges, had retired two years before.

He was now confined to his house with rheumatism which prevented him from walking, and a deafness which prevented him from hearing anything they said to him.

"The ol' place be in rack and ruin!" Shenda had heard one of the estate workers say to her father only last week.

"It is because of the war," the vicar had replied.

"War, or no war, Oi be sick to death of patchin' up moi walls, an' th' thatch on moi roof be in bad shape an' all."

The Vicar sighed, but there was nothing he could do about it.

Shenda knew that the war had meant a great deal of privation and misery for everybody.

What her father missed more than anything else

was not being able to hunt, as he always had, in the winter.

He had, in fact, in the past been known as "The Hunting Parson."

But the gentlemen who contributed towards the foxhounds were either taking an active part in the war, or were so hard up that they could not keep them going as they had in the past.

The Vicar had only two horses left in the stables, and one was so old that Shenda found it quicker to walk than to crawl along on old Snowball's back.

She did not mind walking, especially when it was in the woods.

Now her feet seemed to float over the green moss, and the sunshine percolating through the boughs of the trees turned her hair to gold.

It was then suddenly that she heard Rufus scream and she came back from her dream-world to realise he was not beside her.

He was somewhere ahead in the distance, and as he went on screaming, she ran as swiftly as she could towards him.

As she did so she wondered frantically what could have happened.

He was such a good little dog and never barked when her father was working in his Study and she told him not to.

But she recognised the noise he was making now was a cry of pain.

She found him underneath an ancient elm-tree and saw with horror that his paw was caught in a trap.

There had never been traps in the woods at Arrow,

and she knelt down beside Rufus, who was no longer screaming, but whimpering piteously.

She saw the trap was a new one, and its sharp, tooth-like jaws had imprisoned Rufus's front paw.

Desperately Shenda tried to force it open, but it was too stiff for her and she knew she must get help.

She patted Rufus, talking to him in her soft voice.

She told him that he was not to move until she came back and that she was going to find somebody to help him.

Because he had been with her almost all his life he seemed to understand what she was saying.

Only as she rose to her feet did he whine miserably, but she saw with relief that he did not attempt to follow her.

She then ran as quickly as she could back the way she had come.

She realised it was quite a distance to the village, and she was wondering whom she could find to help her.

At this time of the day, most of the able-bodied men were at work, and there would be only women in the cottages.

She thought of her father, but he had left early that morning to visit an elderly lady who lived nearly two miles away who had sent him an urgent message to say that she was dying.

Because this had happened several times before, Shenda had been rather sceptical whether her father's journey was as urgent as it appeared to be.

Because he was such a handsome, charming man, she knew only too well that a great number of women made any excuse to send for him.

They enjoyed a quiet talk with a man ˅
always courteous and unfailingly sympathetic.

"If I am not back for luncheon," he had said
fore he left, "do not worry."

"I have already prepared myself for having lunch
eon alone," Shenda answered. "You know that Mrs.
Newcomb will 'kill the fatted calf' or whatever is
appropriate, and you might as well enjoy the luxury
of good food while you have the chance!"

Her father laughed.

"I am not saying I shall not enjoy Mrs. Newcomb's food," he said, "but I shall pay for it by listening to her unending list of ailments, both spiritual
and physical."

Shenda put her arm round his neck.

"I love you, Papa," she said, "when you say
things like that. It always used to make Mama
laugh."

Her father kissed her, and she saw the pain in his
eyes when she spoke of her mother, and thought she
had been tactless to remind him of her.

It was impossible to think that any two people
could be happier than The Honourable James Lynd
and his beautiful wife, Doreen.

They had been married after months of opposition
from both of their families.

But despite every gloomy prediction that it was
something they would regret, they had been ecstati-
cally happy.

James was the third son of an impoverished Peer
who had an unproductive estate in the wilds of Gloucestershire.

He had skimped and saved for his oldest son to go

egiment in which he himself had served.

second son was a cripple from birth and was
ng but a liability, and an expensive one.

The only thing he could offer his third son, James,
was a Church on his estate with such a small stipend
that it was almost an insult.

James and Doreen had felt that nothing was important besides their admiration for each other, and
they had moved into the small, uncomfortable Vicarage and filled it with love.

Only when Shenda was born did they become a
little more practical.

James went to see the Bishop, who offered him
the parish of Arrowhead.

He explained that the Earl of Arrow could afford
to give the incumbents under his patronage a good
stipend.

James and Doreen had been delighted with their
new home.

It was a small Elizabethan house, very attractive
to look at, and in good repair.

Because James was not only a Gentleman but also
an excellent horseman, he had been welcomed into
the County, and the future had seemed golden.

Then the war had come, and everything had
changed.

Things were a little better, but only a very little,
during the uneasy Armistice of 1802.

But hostilities broke out again, and there were
more problems and less money, and everything was
more expensive.

Shenda's mother had died after a long, cold winter

when quite unexpectedly she had contracte~~d~~
nia.

It seemed to Shenda as if one moment her m~~~~
was there, smiling and laughing, and the next min~~~~
she was carried to the Churchyard with all the villag~~~~
weeping because she had left them.

Shenda had tried very hard in the last two years to
make her father comfortable, if not happy.

Yet every day it seemed to grow more and more
difficult, and there was less money to spend on food.

Besides which, her father could not help being
over-generous to those in trouble, as he had always
been in the past.

"The Master'd give away th' shirt off 'is back if
anyone asked for it!" one of the servants had said
tartly to Shenda.

She knew this was true, and while she remon-
strated with her father, she knew he was not listening.

"I can hardly let the poor man starve!" he would
say when she pressed him too hard.

"It is not Ned, the artful old beggar, who will
starve, Papa, but you and me!"

"I am sure we can manage, darling," he would
say, and then help somebody else.

She worried about him because he had gone out in
all weathers during the winter, and had developed a
persistent cough which kept him awake at night.

She made him the herb and honey drink her
mother had always advocated, but nothing seemed to
make it any better.

She knew what he really needed was three square

...ay, which was something they could not

"...rhaps when the new Earl comes back," she ...said to old Martha, who was the only servant left ...the Vicarage, "he will realise the wages have to be ...aised, to keep up with the rising prices, and Papa just cannot manage on his stipend!"

"If 'e don't come back 'til the end o' the war," Martha replied, "then we'll be in our graves wi' no-one to mourn us! It's that 'Boney,' that's who it is!"

It was true, Shenda thought, that Bonaparte was to blame for everything that had happened in Arrow-head.

It was "Boney" who made two men come home wounded, one without a leg, the other minus an arm, and "Boney" who had emptied the larder at the Vic-arage.

'If I cannot ask Papa for help, where can I go to find a man to help me?' Shenda thought now.

Then, before she reached the end of the wood she saw to her surprise a man on horseback coming to-wards her.

She realised he was a Gentleman and was moving slowly, talking his horse between the trees, and she ran on until she reached his side.

Looking up at him, she saw that he was fairly young, his high hat at an angle on his dark hair, his white cravat tied in an intricate fashion, and the points of his collar high above his chin.

There was, however, only time to be thankful that he was there.

"Help me!" she said breathlessly, finding it diffi-cult to speak because she had run so quickly.

She saw the Gentleman's eyes travel over her hair which was curling over her forehead.

Then, as she saw he was listening, she said:

"Quickly! Please . . . come . . . quickly! My dog is . . . caught in a . . . trap!"

The Gentleman raised his eye-brows at the urgency with which she spoke, but she did not wait for him to reply. She only said:

"Follow . . . me!"

She ran back the way she had come along the mossy path, where Rufus was waiting.

He was lying still, but whining in a miserable fashion. As she flung herself down beside him, she was aware that the Gentleman had pulled in his horse and was dismounting a little way behind her.

He came to where she was and, looking down, said:

"Be careful, the dog may bite you!"

It was the first words he had spoken, and she answered indignantly:

"Rufus will not bite me. Please , open that . . . terrible trap! It should . . . not be here!"

As she spoke she held Rufus steady and the Gentleman bent down and pulled the teeth of the trap apart.

Rufus gave one yelp of pain, then Shenda was cradling him in her arms as if he were a baby.

"It is all right, it is all over now!" she said softly. "It will not hurt you any more, and you have been a very brave boy!"

As she spoke she was tickling him behind the ears, which Rufus always loved.

Then she was aware that the Gentleman had taken

a handkerchief from his pocket and had gone down on one knee beside her to bandage Rufus's paw.

Shenda looked at him and now, because he was beside her, she could see him more clearly.

"Thank you, thank you!" she said. "I am so very grateful! I was wondering . . . desperately where I could find . . . a man to help me!"

"There must surely be men in the village?" the Gentleman said with a twist of his lips.

"Not at this time of the day," Shenda answered. "They are all at work."

"Then I am glad I was able to be of assistance."

"I cannot . . . thank you . . . enough!" Shenda said. "But how could anybody put that . . . wicked . . . ghastly trap in the wood. There has never been one here before!"

"I suppose it is one way to get rid of the vermin!" the Gentleman replied.

"A very cruel way!" Shenda said. "If any animal gets caught, it could suffer for hours, if not days, before anyone finds it."

The Gentleman did not reply, and she said, almost as if she were speaking to herself:

"How can anyone wish to . . . create more . . . suffering when there is so much of it in the world . . . already?"

"I suppose you are thinking of the war," the Gentleman remarked. "All wars are wrong, but we are fighting to defend our country."

"To kill an animal . . . unless it is to feed someone . . . cannot be . . . right!"

"I can see you are a Reformer," the Gentleman remarked, "but animals prey on each other. Too

12

many foxes, if they are not hunted, kill the rabbits, which I am sure you think are very pretty."

She realised he was mocking at her, and there was a faint flush on her cheeks as she said:

"Nature, if left alone, will create a balance of its own, and I cannot bear to think of foxes suffering hours of agony or even rabbits struggling in a snare until they hang themselves!"

"That is a woman's point of view," the Gentleman argued, "and if one wants to preserve game, then those who prey on the birds have to be accounted for."

He spoke in a crisp, dry voice, and because Shenda thought it would be hopeless to argue with him, she said:

"To me, this wood has always been a magical... beautiful place, and now, if I am to be barred from coming into it by traps and cruelty, it will be like being... turned out of... Paradise!"

She was speaking to herself more than to the Gentleman.

Then, as she was afraid he might laugh at her, she got carefully to her feet holding Rufus close against her and said:

"Once again, Sir, thank you very much for your assistance, and now I must take Rufus home and have his paw washed in case it becomes poisoned."

She looked at the trap as she spoke, then added:

"I wonder if... you would do... me one more ... kindness?"

"What is that?" the Gentleman asked.

"Just a little bit farther on is a magic pool. If you

13

would throw that trap into it . . . it will never . . . again hurt any . . . living creature."

"You do not think the owner of the trap, having paid quite a considerable sum for it, might object?"

"He will not know what has happened," Shenda replied, "and if it cost him money to put it there . . . then that is his . . . punishment!"

The Gentleman laughed.

"Very well," he said, "as you have constituted yourself Judge, Jury, and Hangman, the accused must pay the price for his crime!"

He picked up the trap by the chain with which it was pinioned to the ground, and, having pulled it free, asked:

"Now, where is this magical pool?"

"I will show you the way," Shenda said.

She walked ahead and, after passing several large trees, they came to it.

The pool was looking, she thought, even more beautiful than when she had seen it two days previously.

Now there were more kingcups out, more irises, and the sunshine coming through the trees glittered golden on the centre of the pool.

The sides were dark and mysterious, as if they hid secrets which belonged only to the gods.

The Gentleman went to the side of the pool and stood looking down at it.

Then he half-turned to look at Shenda, who was standing beside him.

With the yellow irises touching her gown and the trees behind her, she made a picture which any artist would have found entrancing.

Her eyes seemed to fill her small, pointed face, but instead of being the blue that was usually associated with the gold of her hair, they were a soft grey.

Yet in some lights they had an almost purple tinge.

It was a characteristic that was prevalent in her mother's family.

With the whiteness of her skin which never seemed to be tanned by the sun, she had an ethereal beauty that was very different from what was admired as the "perfect English Rose."

Instead, she seemed part of the woods and the mystery of the pool, and the sunlight on the buds of the ancient trees.

For a moment Shenda and the Gentleman just looked at each other.

If he thought that she was unbelievably lovely and hardly human, to her he was very handsome.

His skin was brown, as if he had been a long time in the sun, and his features were well-formed.

Yet, she thought, good-looking though he was, there was something hard about him, something which made her feel, although she could not explain it, as if he were used to giving commands.

He seemed to have a strength that came not only from his athletic body, but also from his mind.

Then, as if he wanted to break the spell which had kept them both silent, he said abruptly:

"Do you want the trap thrown into the centre of the pool?"

"It is deeper there, I think, than anywhere else."

He swung the trap by its chain, then let it go.

It fell with a splash and the water was thrown

iridescent into the air before it settled once again into an unrippled silver stillness.

Shenda gave a deep sigh.

"Thank you very much," she said, "and now I must take Rufus home."

She looked again at the pool, and it was almost as if she embraced it.

Then she turned resolutely away and started back the way they had come.

The Gentleman's horse was still where he had left it, cropping the undergrowth for small blades of grass.

He caught it by the bridle and said:

"As you have your dog to carry, I will take you home on my saddle."

Shenda was surprised, but without saying any more he picked her up in his arms and set her on the saddle.

Then, taking his horse's bridle, he led it onto the mossy path.

They moved in silence until, as the wood came to an end, Shenda could see the Vicarage garden ahead of her.

She suddenly thought it would be a mistake for anybody in the village to see her with a strange Gentleman, or to learn that Rufus had been caught in a trap.

It would cause a great deal of comment if anybody were aware that a stranger had carried her on the saddle of his horse.

"Please, Sir," she said, speaking softly, "as my home is now just ahead of us . . . I would like to . . . get down."

The Gentleman drew his horse to a standstill.

Then, when Shenda would have slipped to the ground, he lifted her down with the same ease as when he had put her into the saddle.

She was very light, and her waist was so small that his fingers almost met round it.

As her feet touched the ground she said:

"Thank you once again! I am very . . . very grateful, and I will never . . . forget your . . . kindness!"

"What is your name?" he asked.

"Shenda," she replied without thinking.

He swept his hat from his head.

"Then, good-bye, Shenda, and I feel sure, as we have destroyed what is wrong and disturbing in your magical world, that you will be able to go there again without fear."

"I . . . I hope . . . so," she answered.

She thought there was something more she ought to say, then, as she hesitated, he said quietly:

"If you are really grateful for the small service I have been able to do for you, I think you should reward me for my labours."

She looked at him in a puzzled fashion, not understanding what he was saying.

Then he put his fingers under her chin, turned her face up to his, and kissed her.

She was so astonished that she was unable to move.

It was a very gentle kiss, and as he released her, he mounted his horse.

Before she could speak or move, he had ridden away.

As she watched him disappearing through the

trees she thought she must be dreaming.

How could she possibly have been kissed for the first time in her life by a total stranger she had never seen before, and who was trespassing in what she thought of as her own wood?

It was only a few seconds before he was out of sight between the trees.

Yet still she stood there, thinking he had disappeared so quickly that she must have dreamt the whole episode and it was something that had not really happened.

But she could still feel the touch of his lips on hers, and although it seemed incredible, he had actually kissed her!

Rufus whined, and the sound brought her back to reality.

Holding the little dog close against her breast, she ran through what was left of the trees before they joined the shrubs in the Vicarage garden.

There was a path she always used which led her to the side of the house where there was what was always known as the "Garden Door."

She hurried through it, feeling as she did so that she had stepped back into her ordinary life.

There was Rufus's paw to be seen to, and the sooner she forgot what had happened, the better.

Then she knew, as she moved down the passage which led to the Kitchen on the other side of the house, that it was something she would never forget.

There was no-one in the Kitchen because Martha had come and gone.

She came in the mornings to tidy up and prepare the luncheon, then would go back to her own cottage, where she lived with her son, who was the village "looney."

Having looked after him, she would then return to cook the dinner for Shenda and her father.

Martha was a good cook because she had served her apprenticeship at the Castle when she was a girl, but she had to have the right ingredients.

As Shenda was aware, it was difficult to buy the good meat which her father enjoyed without sufficient money to pay for it.

She knew that Martha would have left early today because she would be alone for luncheon, and there would be just something cold on a plate with a salad and the few vegetables that were to be found in the garden.

She put Rufus down on the kitchen table which Martha scrubbed every day.

As she did so she was aware that the Gentleman's handkerchief, which was now stained with blood, was still around Rufus's paw.

It was an expensive handkerchief, of fine linen, and Shenda thought with a smile that it was unlikely she would be able to return it to its owner.

He had asked her name, but she had not asked his.

"It is unimportant, as I shall never see him again," she told herself.

She thought perhaps he was a visitor to one of the large houses in the neighbourhood.

There were a few elderly people whose sons were at the war, but who had given up entertaining, although, when her mother had been alive, she and her father had sometimes been invited out to dinner.

She was thinking it over, but the handsome Gentleman with the smart clothes did not seem somehow to fit in.

"Then I *must* have dreamt him!" Shenda said to herself with a smile as she washed the little dog's paw, Rufus whining only when she hurt him.

She found some strips of clean linen in a drawer in the Kitchen.

She was just about to put the handkerchief into cold water to soak away the blood-stains when there was a heavy knock on the Kitchen door.

"Come in!" she called, thinking it was somebody from the village.

The door opened and she saw it was the large son of a Farmer.

"Good-morning, Jim!" she said pleasantly. "What can I do for you?"

"It be bad news, Miss Shenda!" he said.

Shenda was still.

"What has . . . happened?"

"It's yer faither, Miss, but it weren't our fault. We'd thought as 'ow the bull'd be in that field!"

"Bull? What has happened?" Shenda asked in a voice that did not sound like her own.

"That there bull, 'e knocked t'Vicar off 'n 'is 'orse, Miss Shenda, an' Oi thinks as 'ow 'e's killt 'im!"

Shenda gave a cry.

"Oh, no! It cannot be true!"

"It be, Miss. Me faither and t'other men be a-bringin' 'im 'ome on a gate!"

With an effort Shenda put Rufus, who was still standing on the table, down on the floor.

Then, as she walked from the Kitchen preparatory to going into the hall to open the front-door, Jim followed her, saying over and over again:

"T'weren't our fault, Miss Shenda. Us thought as 'ow no-one'd go into that field!"

chapter two

DRIVING towards the Admiralty, the Earl of Arrow thought with admiration of the Prime Minister.

In defiance of the Cabinet and a great number of the Members of Parliament, William Pitt had appointed a man of his own choice to be First Lord.

In the Earl's opinion, no-one could have been a better choice than Admiral Sir Charles Middleton, now Lord Barham.

Those who remembered him before he retired knew that he was the greatest Naval Administrator since Samuel Pepys.

After Viscount Melville was forced to resign, owing to a charge of malpractice concerning his Department, there had been a great number of applicants for the position, favoured not only by the Cabinet but also the Opposition.

During the winter the Prime Minister had been

struggling to form a Continental Coalition in the face of endless difficulties.

There was the greed of potential allies for subsidies, fear of France, icebound roads that held up couriers for weeks, wildly unrealistic Russian hopes of Spanish collaboration, and the inability of foreign powers to understand the nature and limitations of British sea power.

The Prime Minister faced these obstacles with courage.

He had run the gauntlet of the Opposition wits with a new bill to draft militiamen into the Army, aiming thereby to recruit 17,000 Regulars.

Meanwhile, he scraped together every man who could be sent out of England, and by March, 5,000 had been ready to set sail for India.

The Earl was aware of a great deal of this, and he had an enormous respect for the Prime Minister.

Yet, as a sailor, he was well aware that the only real defence of England lay in her Navy.

When he reached the Admiralty he found he was expected, and was shown immediately into the office, where Lord Barham was waiting for him.

He rose as the Earl entered and was certainly looking hale and hearty and nowhere near his seventy-eight years of age.

The Prince of Wales and the Whigs who had opposed his appointment had announced that he was eighty-two and made great sport of it.

Lord Barham held out his hand.

"Arrow!" he exclaimed. "I cannot tell you how delighted I am to see you!"

"I came as quickly as I could," the Earl replied, "but it was hard to give up my ship."

"I knew you would feel that way," Lord Barham said, "and I have to congratulate you, not only on being the youngest Captain in the British Navy, but on your achievements. There is no need for me to enumerate them."

"None!" the Earl replied.

He sat down in the comfortable chair indicated by Lord Barham and said with just a touch of anxiety in his voice:

"Now, what is this all about? I knew I had to come home once I had inherited the title and my father's estates, but I did not expect so much hurry over it."

"I wanted you," Lord Barham said briefly.

The Earl raised his eye-brows, and Lord Barham continued:

"I know of no-one, and this is the truth, Arrow, who could help me as well as you can do at this present moment."

The Earl was listening, but he did not speak as Lord Barham went on:

"Not by coming to the Admiralty, which I know would be something you would dislike, but by assisting me without anybody being aware of it in the Social World which you have now entered."

The Earl's expression, which had been one of curiosity tinged with anxiety, changed.

He had been afraid when he had received a command from the Admiralty to return with his ship which had been blockading the French at Toulon, that he was to be forced into the position of what he called an "Office Clerk."

He had intended to oppose this appointment by every means in his power, and it was a relief to realise that that was not what was in Lord Barham's mind.

The First Lord sat down in a chair next to his and said:

"I have come to the Admiralty to find the muddle I expected, because, as you are well aware without my being unkind, Henry Dundas, or Viscount Melville as he now is, made a mess of the Royal Commission's Report on Naval expenditure."

The Earl nodded, and Lord Barham went on:

"He treated the Commission with scant respect, and it avenged itself by exposing certain malpractices committed under his rule ten years ago."

"I heard something of the sort," the Earl answered, "but of course, news from England arrived in a haphazard manner, which made it difficult to follow the political situation."

"Melville had to resign, and I am in his place," Lord Barham said, "and now those who oppose me are waiting for me to make a fool of myself."

"That is certainly something you must not do!" the Earl replied.

"Now, where I need your help," Lord Barham went on briskly, "is in discovering the leaks that are taking place in the Admiralty! Bonaparte's spies are everywhere, even, I believe, in Carlton House!"

The Earl sat upright in his chair.

"Are you sure of this?" he asked incredulously.

"Very sure," Lord Barham said. "Napoleon knows what we are doing almost as soon as we do ourselves, and it is a situation which cannot continue."

"Of course not!" the Earl agreed.

"What I want you to do is comparatively easy," Lord Braham said. "You are now a man of Social importance, and the Prince of Wales will be eager to make you his friend."

There was a twinkle in his eye as he said:

"Your exploits against the French will undoubtedly amuse him, but make sure he hears about them before you tell anybody else."

He saw the expression on the Earl's face and knew that he had no wish to boast of his achievements.

"This is not a moment for false modesty," Lord Barham said, "and everything you do will have a reason behind it, and will be very much a part of my plan for beating Napoleon!"

"I can only pray that is what you will do!" the Earl said sincerely.

"It is certainly not going to be easy," Lord Barham replied. "And now I am going to trust you with a secret that must be prevented at all costs from reaching France."

The Earl sat forward in his chair and Lord Barham continued:

"A large and very important force of soldiers has been concentrated at Portsmouth under Lieutenant-General Sir James Craig. It will proceed—I quote—'on a foreign expedition going no-one knows whither.'"

The Earl was listening intently as Lord Barham went on, still in a low voice:

"With commendable spirit, the Prime Minister, disregarding the possibility of invasion of this island, is preparing to launch this Army into the unknown."

"That is what I would expect of him," the Earl said in a tone of admiration.

"In front of what we call the 'Secret Expedition,'" Lord Barham went on, "is a twenty-five-hundred-mile voyage pasts Ports containing five undefeated enemy Fleets of nearly seventy ships of the line."

There was no need for him to elaborate to the Earl, who had just come back to England, the dangers that awaited such a journey.

"What I am going to tell you," he said, "is something which is not known to anybody—not even in this office—except myself. They are Craig's embarkation orders!"

Knowing how secret this was, the Earl, with difficulty, prevented himself from looking over his shoulder as if afraid somebody might be eavesdropping.

"He is to proceed to Malta," Lord Barham went on, "freeing eight thousand troops already there for offensive operations, to co-operate with a Russian Force from Corfu for the liberation of the Neapolitan mainlaind and the defence of Sicily."

He was aware that the Earl was staring at him almost incredulously, and said:

"If necessary, since its security is essential to England's European plan, he is to garrison the island without the consent of the King, and is also, with Nelson's aid, to safeguard Egypt and Sardinia."

He ceased speaking and the Earl said:

"I can only say I am astounded! But I can understand, knowing the terrifying dangers of the voyage, that 'Secret Expedition' is the right description for it!"

He also thought with a faint smile that on board the packed ships expectation would be running high as, after many months of inaction, the Army was at last to have its chance.

"To finish my story," Lord Barham said, "two days ago, on April nineteenth, the wind which has held up the forty-five transports from leaving England changed, and they stood out to sea escorted by two first rates."

"And you really think," the Earl asked, "that this can be kept a close secret?"

"I am told Napolean's spies have been active," Lord Barham said, "but my reports are that they have no idea of where the expedition is going. In fact, one reliable source says that Bonaparte himself believes it is destined for the West Indies."

"In which case he will send what ships he has to attack them!" the Earl said.

"Of course!" Lord Barham agreed. "And as he is certain of his impending mastery of the world, he must scare Downing Street into dispersing its slender military forces."

"I can see the whole picture," the Earl said. "At the same time, I am not quite certain how I come into this."

"Use your brain, my dear boy," Lord Barham replied. "Spies, as you well know, are not sinister-looking men in dark clothes lurking in alley-ways. They are often a pair of pleading eyes and pouting lips with a penchant for diamonds!"

The Earl frowned.

"Are you seriously telling me there are women in England who would spy for France?"

"Willingly or unwillingly, intentionally or unintentionally, I am certain that is happening," Lord Barham said, "and as you know only too well, Arrow, a careless word murmured into a shell-like ear on the pillow can mean the death of men carrying the British flag in a far-off country, or the sinking of a ship which is fatal at the moment to our defence."

The Earl's lips tightened and he said:

"I know exactly what you are saying, and I nearly lost my own ship two months ago because somebody alerted the enemy that we were approaching, and only by the mercy of God were we saved at the last moment!"

"Then you understand what I am asking of you," Lord Barham said.

He threw out his hand expressively as he said:

"Circulate amongst His Royal Highness's cronies who flock like hungry crows to Carlton House. Call on the great hostesses, both Tory and Whig, and keep your ears open and your brain clear."

"I may prove a dismal failure," the Earl said. "I am at home on a bridge, and can handle a ship better than a woman!"

Lord Barham laughed.

"I was quite certain you had been at sea too long! And now, forget the clever exploits of Captain Durwin Bow, and concentrate on being an Earl who has little on his mind except to enjoy himself!"

The Earl sighed.

"I think I would almost rather be the desk-bound

Clerk I expected to be when you sent for me!"

"That, my boy, would be a waste of your talents, your looks, and your position!"

Lord Barham laughed before he said:

"No-one would expect an Earl to be a spy, but that is exactly what you have to be, and I can only beg of you to realise that the lives of seven thousand troops depend on you, apart from the fact that, unless they reach their destination, the Prime Minister will have more trouble with the Russians than he has had already."

"Then all I can reply is that I will do my damnedest!" the Earl said.

"That is the only answer I want." Lord Barham smiled.

He rose as he spoke and the Earl realised that the interview was at an end.

"Do not come to see me again unless you have something of import to impart," Lord Barham ended. "Put nothing in writing, and trust no-one in this office, or outside it."

"You are making my flesh creep!" the Earl complained.

"That is what I want to do," Lord Barham said. "There has been too much complacency up until now, and that is something, I assure you, we cannot afford!"

He paused, then he added:

"Incidentally, nothing has been heard of Nelson, a somewhat erratic young Admiral in my view!"

"You have no idea where he is?" the Earl asked incredulously.

"None!" Lord Barham said briefly. "And if his

only eye has once more carried him off to Egypt, the Government will find themselves 'in a scrape.'"

"Why?" the Earl enquired.

"It is important for Nelson to maintain control of the central Mediterranean," Lord Barham answered.

"I thought he had done that so successfully that the French Fleet had abandoned that Sea altogether, and gone buccaneering in the Atlantic."

"That is what we had hoped," Lord Barham said, "but now Nelson has vanished, and no-one seems to know where!"

"I am quite certain that whatever he does will be the right thing," the Earl said quietly.

He thought Lord Barham was slightly sceptical at his optimistic remark, but he did not say so.

He merely took the Earl to the door and, opening it, said in a loud voice that could be heard by everybody in the outer office:

"It has been delightful to see you, my dear boy. We shall miss you in the Navy, but I do understand you have a great deal to do on your estates. Take time off to enjoy yourself after all your hard work!"

He shook the Earl by the hand, then one of the Senior Clerks escorted him to the front-door.

The First Lord went back to his own office with the air of a man who had wasted too much time for no good reason.

The Earl climbed into his Phaeton, thinking how he could even begin to carry out Lord Barham's orders.

He had, however, a very astute brain.

There had been no need for the First Lord to impress on him more than he had done already the importance of the Secret Expedition and the danger of Napoleon's spies having infiltrated the *Beau Ton*.

Every country had spies, the Earl was well aware of that.

But that Napoleon should have been clever enough to make them men and women who were accepted by the great hostesses, by the Prince of Wales and perhaps at Buckingham Palace, was something he had not thought of in the past.

He was, however, aware that there were a great many *émigrés* in England who had come to the country for sanctuary during the French Revolution.

In a number of cases, as their *Châteaux* and estates had been looted or confiscated, they had not returned even when Napoleon invited them to do so.

They might constitute a danger but, at the same time, the Earl knew they professed a loathing for the "Corsican Upstart" who had come to power entirely through the Revolution and had now crowned himself Emperor.

They were affronted when they were told how he had installed himself in the Royal Palaces and was behaving more royally than Charlemagne.

"Could there be spies amongst the *émigrés*?" the Earl asked himself. "If not, then who else?"

He drove his Phaeton up the Mall, past St. James's Palace and into St. James's Street.

As he did so he thought now that he was back in England that he would go to Whites, the Club where he was certain he would find the majority of his friends.

He would also, he was well aware, hear the latest gossip.

Perhaps, although it seemed unlikely, that would give him a clue as to where he should look for the despicable creatures who were ready to debase themselves by taking money from the French.

He drew up outside the Club and, walking in, was not really surprised when the Head Porter said:

"Good-day, M'Lord! It's nice to see you back after so many years!"

The Earl laughed.

It was part of the tradition of Whites that the Porters should know and remember the members.

He was a clearly aware, too, that he was no longer Lieutenant-Commander Bow, as he had been the last time he entered the Club, but was now the Earl of Arrow.

"I am glad to be back, Johnson," he said.

He was gratified not only by the Porter's appreciation of him in remembering his name, but also by his own memory.

"You'll find Captain Crawshore in the Morning-Room, M'Lord," Johnson said.

The Earl was amused, too, that the porter even remembered his friends.

He walked into the Morning-Room, and for a moment there seemed to be a pause in the conversation as the members looked at him.

Then there was a cry of: "Durwin!" and a second later Perry Crawshore was beside him.

"You are home!" he said, wringing his hands. "I was wondering when you would get back!"

"I arrived a few days ago," the Earl replied, "and I went first to my house in Berkeley Square, which is in the hell of a mess."

"I would have helped you if you had asked me," Perry said.

"I am asking you now," the Earl replied.

He sat down in one of the leather armchairs beside his friend and told a Club servant to bring him a drink.

"Now that you are back, what are you going to do?" Perry asked.

"Enjoy myself!" the Earl replied. "I have been rocking on the sea for so many months that I began to think I should never be able to stand steady on *terra firma* again!"

"Are you going to stay in London, or go to the country?" Perry asked.

"Both!" the Earl replied. "And I am looking to you, Perry, to introduce me to all the Beauties and the 'Incomparables,' as if I were an innocent *débutante*!"

Perry Crawshore shouted with laughter, and two or three other men who knew the Earl in the past came up to ask where he had been.

"We thought you have been swallowed by a sea-lion, or eloped with a pretty mermaid!" one of them quipped.

"If there are any mermaids in the Mediterranean, I have not seen one!" the Earl replied. "And the porpoises are more of a nuisance than the French!"

"How long is this damned war going to continue?" somebody asked.

It seemed to the Earl that everybody looked at him, and after a moment he said:

"Until Napoleon is defeated, and make no mis-

take, there is no-one who can do that except ourselves!"

*   *   *

Shenda looked around the house that had been her
home ever since she could remember, and found it
difficult to believe she now had to leave it.

When she had received a letter from the man who
had just been appointed Manager to the Arrow Estate
asking her to vacate the Vicarage within two weeks,
she had sat down and cried.

The only person she could go to was her father's
older brother who had, on her grandfather's death,
moved into the house in Gloucestershire.

She had met him twice in the last two years and
had thought he was very unlike her father.

He was also, she knew, exceedingly hard-up since
he left the Army. He had four children of his own
and had great difficulty in making ends meet.

"How can I possibly impose myself on him?" she
asked.

But there was nowhere else she could go.

She had never met her mother's relatives who
lived in the North of Scotland, and had known from
what her mother had told her that they had always
disapproved of her father.

While she packed her clothes and the things she
wished to keep, she had been turning over and over
in her mind the desperate problem of her future.

There was no use pretending she had any money
because all she had was the few pounds she had obtained for selling some of the furniture not worth
storing.

Farmer Johnson, however, whose bull had killed her father, had offered to look after anything she might leave with him at the farm.

"Ye can 'ave one 'o the Out-houses, Miss Shenda," he said, "or there's th' attic, if ye prefers. Oi'll see they comes to no 'arm, ye can be sure o' that!"

"That is very kind of you," Shenda replied, "but there is not much, only a few trunks, and perhaps two or three packing cases."

"Oi'll send Jim wi' t'cart to carry 'em back up 'ere," the Farmer said, "an' ye know, Miss Shenda, anythin' we does for ye, we does willin'!"

She knew he felt guilty because his bull had killed her father, though it was really nobody's fault.

How could her father have known that a particularly savage bull was in the field he always crossed when he visited Mrs. Newcomb?

How could Farmer Johnson know that it was the Vicar's normal custom, for he had never bothered to tell him.

There was a packing-case that was still half-empty, and as Shenda looked at it she remembered that one of her mother's special tablecloths had been left in a cupboard in the Dining-Room.

She went to fetch it, and as she took it from the shelf she saw there was a tear in the lace which decorated the edges and knew it should have been mended.

Her mother had taught her to sew as neatly as she did herself.

Shenda could also repair lace and other materials

with such tiny stitches that everyone in the village admired her work.

She picked up the cloth and, wrapping it in white paper, laid it carefully in the packing-case.

As she did so she wondered if she would ever again have a home of her own where she could use the things which once had seemed quite ordinary because they were part of the way they lived, but were now luxuries.

Then, as she patted the cloth almost as if she were caressing it, she had a sudden idea, an idea that she felt must have come in some way from her mother.

Only last night she had lain in bed praying first to God, then to her mother for help.

"What shall I do, Mama?" she asked. "I am sure Uncle William does not want another mouth to feed, and if I go there and take Rufus with me, that will mean two mouths."

She knew as she prayed that the one thing she could not bear to lose was Rufus.

She had the uncomfortable feeling at the back of her mind that her aunt, who she thought had looked at her in a somewhat hostile manner, would not want a dog in the house.

"Help me . . . Mama . . . help . . . me!" she prayed desperately.

Because she spoke aloud without meaning to, Rufus had crept up to the bed to comfort her.

She held him in her arms, aware as she did so that his paw had healed.

He still, however, walked delicately, as if he were afraid that every time he touched the ground it would hurt him.

37

Her fingers lingered on him, and he raised his paw, as if he were speaking to her.

She ran up to her almost empty bedroom to get her bonnet.

"Come, Rufus!" she called. "We are going for a walk!"

With the spaniel at her heels, she went through the garden that was now a kaleidoscope of colours, and then into the wood.

She did not, however, take the mossy path that led to the magic pool, but instead set off across the Park in the direction of the Castle.

It looked very imposing with its ancient tower pointing towards the sky.

The rest of the house which had been added generation after generation was silhouetted against the woods that lay at the back of it.

If the Vicarage garden was a bower of beauty, the garden of the Castle was, Shenda thought, lovelier every time she saw it.

It was especially lovely in the Spring, and now the almond trees were in bloom and the box-hedges protecting the formal gardens which had been first laid out in the reign of Elizabeth were neatly trimmed.

All through the late Earl's illness, the gardeners had kept the garden as beautiful as if they thought that, at any moment, he might come out to inspect it.

Shenda had often thought it must be disappointing for them that he would not do so.

Whenever she visited the Castle on one pretext or another, she would tell old Hodges, the Head Gardener, how beautiful they had made it.

She felt that, because she praised him, he looked forward to seeing her.

There was a cascade, a fountain, a bowling-green, an Herb-Garden, and a dozen other places which delighted her eyes and fired her imagination.

She would tell herself stories of those who had lived at the Castle, particularly the one of the first Knight.

A battle had taken place in medieval times and the Commander, whose name was Hlodwig, had with his men attacked the Danes who had landed to pillage and plunder with a stronger force than his own.

The battle was going against them when, taking a bow from one of his soldiers, he shot the arrow himself, killing the leader of the Danes.

He had been rewarded by being made a Knight and became Sir Justin Bow.

He had moved inland and built a fortified Manor House, most appropriately calling it "Arrow."

The Earldom had been created in the reign of Charles II with the title of Arrow.

All through history the Bows had served in the Army and Navy, and also as advisers to the Monarch.

It was such a romantic story that Shenda would imagine the Castle filled first with Knights in armour, their ladies wearing long, pointed medieval head-dresses.

Then there were the doublets and ruffs of Tudor times, and the long wigs which emulated the one worn by Charles II after the Restoration.

In her mind Shenda designed herself a gown to go with the period and wished she could have one in the present fashion which had swept England from France after it had been introduced by the Empress Josephine.

She knew that the thin, almost transparent gauze or muslin dress with its high waist, puff sleeves, and ribbons crossed over the breast, would suit her.

Then, as she reached the Castle, she laughed at the idea, knowing that what concerned her at the moment was not having a new gown, but enough to eat.

She went to the main door automatically and only when it was opened by a new servant she had not seen before did she think perhaps she should have gone to the Kitchen entrance.

"I wish to see Mrs. Davison," she said in her soft voice.

She was sure the servant was thinking, as she had, that it was the wrong door to ask for the House-keeper, but he merely replied:

"I'll find out if she'll see you. What name shall I say?"

"Miss Lynd," Shenda replied. "I come from the Vicarage."

Now the servant's attitude changed.

"If you'll come upstairs, Miss," he said, "I'll take you to Mrs. Davison's room."

"Thank you," Shenda answered.

She had expected that the new Earl would engage more servants, as the household had been sadly depleted in the last two years.

She hoped only he had not dispensed with the older ones whom she had known all through the long years when the old Earl was too ill to see anyone.

Because it was polite, her father had called almost

every week, and had taken her with him.

Sometimes the Earl would see her father, and she would wait outside in the Gig in which they had arrived.

At others, Bates, the Butler, who had been there for forty years, would ask her to come inside and she would wait in one of the rooms which was kept open for callers.

If it was in the afternoon, Bates would suggest she have a cup of tea in the Morning-Room which Shenda knew was used as a Dining-Room by the family when they stayed overnight.

Every other room in the great house had Holland covers over the furniture, the shutters closed, and the curtains drawn.

It all seemed to her very sad, and she now wanted to ask if the State Rooms had been opened. Then she knew the servant would think she was being too curious.

He knocked at the Housekeeper's door which Shenda could have found quite easily herself, and when Mrs. Davison said, "Come in," he opened it and let Shenda pass him.

Mrs. Davison, who was sitting by the window, gave a cry of delight when she saw her.

"Miss Shenda!" she exclaimed. "I was only thinking about you a little while ago, and wondering what you would be doing after the death of your dear father."

"That is what I came to talk to you about," Shenda replied.

"Oh, my dear, I'm so sorry!" Mrs. Davison said.

Taking Shenda by the hand, she pulled her towards a comfortable armchair and sat down next to it.

"I know what you must feel without your mother, God rest her soul, and your father, whom we all loved."

"There is a new Vicar coming in almost at once!" Shenda said.

"So quickly?" Mrs. Davison exclaimed. "That's the doing of that new Manager. Everything about him is hurry, hurry, and no time to draw breath, and that's a fact!"

"I saw there was a new footman, I suppose that was what he was, who opened the door!" Shenda remarked.

"Four of them! And all wanting training by Mr. Bates, which doesn't please him, I can tell you!"

Then Mrs. Davison smiled.

"Nevertheless, it'll be like old times to have the house open with house-parties, and would you believe it, Miss Shenda, there's a party coming down from London next Friday! Twelve of them!"

"With the new Earl?" Shenda asked.

"Of course!"

It flashed through Shenda's mind that she would like to meet him.

Then she remembered why she had come.

"I have an idea, Mrs. Davison," she said, "and I do not know what you will think about it."

"An idea?" Mrs. Davison said. "If it's as good as the ones your mother used to suggest to me, then I can tell you, I'll welcome it!"

"You are so kind," Shenda said, "but I think first I

must tell you that I have no money and nowhere to go."

Mrs. Davison stared at her.

"I can hardly believe it! What about your relatives?"

"There is only Papa's brother who lives in Gloucestershire, and I feel sure he will not want me, nor will he welcome Rufus!"

She put her hand down as she spoke and touched Rufus, who was lying at her feet.

He had followed her closely all the way up the stairs and now was very quiet and still as she had taught him to be when they were in other people's houses.

"That's the most terrible thing I've ever heard!" Mrs. Davison was saying. "But what's your idea, Miss Shenda?"

"I thought . . . Mrs. Davison . . . that it would be . . . wonderful for me . . . if I could come here . . . as a seamstress!"

Mrs. Davison stared at her, and Shenda went on quickly:

"Mama used to tell me how in the old days when she and the Countess were friends, there was always a seamstress in the Castle."

"Indeed there was!" Mrs. Davison said. "And when she died, oh, eighty she was, and nearly blind, I didn't replace her. I thought with all the rooms closed what was necessary to be done I could do myself. But now things are different."

"You have not engaged anyone?" Shenda asked quickly.

"I've thought about it, I certainly thought about it

when they tells me there's twelve guests arriving in three days' time! And the Ladies of the party'll all have their maids with them, and the Gentlemen their valets."

Mrs. Davison drew in her breath before she added:

"If there's not a lot of torn sheets and pillow-cases without buttons at the end of their visit, then you can call me a liar!"

"I can do all those things, and mend anything else for you!" Shenda said eagerly.

"But you're a Lady, Miss Shenda! You ought to be sitting downstairs with His Lordship's guests—and none of them'll be as lovely as you!"

Shenda laughed.

"Thank you, Mrs. Davison, it is very kind of you to say so, but you know I would be the Beggar Maid at the feast without a decent gown to my name, and no money with which to buy one!"

Then in a different tone she said:

"Please . . . please, Mrs. Davison . . . let me stay! I would be so unhappy away from the village and all the people who knew Mama and Papa. And if I can stay near, it will be like . . . living at home. His Lordship is not likely to meet the seamstress, whether she is the poor old woman who died, or me!"

"That's true," Mrs. Davison said, "and I don't suppose that Mr. Marlow, who's the new Agent'll interfere with the Household."

"Then I may stay? Oh, please, Mrs. Davison . . . I can stay?"

"Of course you can stay, Miss Shenda, if it'll make you happy," Mrs. Davison agreed. "You can have your meals with me, and the Seamstress's Room is on the top floor with a comfortable bedroom next door."

She thought for a moment. Then she said:

"No! I think that'd be a mistake. I'll have you next to me! There are two rooms kept for visiting lady's-maids which I can easily turn into a bedroom and a Sewing-Room, and I shall feel I'm looking after you, so to speak."

"You are so kind . . . so very, very kind!" Shenda said.

There were tears in her eyes as she added:

"I thought I should have to . . . go away and that . . . nobody would . . . want me."

"I want you, Miss Shenda, and that's the truth!" Mrs. Davison said. "Anyway, I was intending to say to His Lordship as soon as I got the chance that I can't manage without help."

"Now you can tell him you have help," Shenda said. "It will be lovely to be here and I can talk to you about Mama and Papa, and not feel I am alone and have left everything that was . . . familiar."

As she spoke, a tear ran down her cheek and she brushed it away with the back of her hand.

"Now, don't you go upsetting yourself," Mrs. Davison said. "What we'll do now is to have a nice cup of tea, and you can tell me what you want to bring with you."

"Farmer Johnson has been very kind and says he will store anything I do not want for the moment," Shenda said, "but it would be lovely to be able to keep my things here. Perhaps you have room in the attics?"

"Room?" Mrs. Davison replied. "There's enough room for furniture from a dozen houses, as well you know! You can keep your things by you, Miss Shenda, knowing they're there if you wants them."

"That will be wonderful!" Shenda said. "And perhaps if you do not have too much work to give me, I could make myself a new gown. I have not been able to afford one for years, and I would not want you to be ashamed of me!"

Mrs. Davison smiled.

"You're exactly like your mother—the most beautiful Lady I've ever seen, and that's the truth, cross m'heart!"

"You could not say anything that would make me happier!" Shenda said. "Oh, Mrs. Davison, thank you, thank you!"

She got up from the chair and impulsively kissed the old Housekeeper.

"Now that's settled!" Mrs. Davison said. "And I know Mr. Bates'll be as pleased as I am that you're safe, and that we can keep an eye on you. There's no need for anybody else, except those who have been here years, like yourselves, to know who you are."

Shenda looked at her enquiringly, and she said:

"The new staff might feel embarrassed seeing you're a Lady, and yet you're employed as they are."

"I understand!" Shenda said. "And of course I will be very tactful."

"What you've to do is to keep out of their way," Mrs. Davison said. "You can have your own Sitting-Room, and your meals with me, and if I like to take them on my own, that's my business and there's no reason for anyone to interfere."

"I will be quite happy on my own if you have to eat in the Housekeeper's Dining-Room," Shenda said.

She knew when the house was full that the top servants ate in what was known as the "Housekeeper's Dining-Room" while the lower and younger servants were in the Servants' Hall.

"Now, you leave everything to me," Mrs. Davison said. "I know what's right, and what your dear mother'd want. I won't have you mixing with those who wouldn't treat you as they should!"

She spoke so positively that Shenda had no wish to argue.

She merely thanked Mrs. Davison again for saving her and Rufus, and said in her heart:

"Thank you, thank you, Mama! I know this was your idea, and now I am safe!"

chapter three

THE Earl was looking forward with pleasure to his first party at the Castle.

Perry had said he must invite the friends he had known in the past, and pair them off with the attractive women with whom they were enamoured at the moment.

Perry was not only excited at having the Earl back from sea, but he thought it important that he should enjoy himself in London after being away for so many years.

"You will have to forget the war now, old boy!" he said. "Everybody is sick of talking about it, and the Prince of Wales has set the pace by amusing himself continuously and extravagantly."

For a moment the Earl could think only of the sufferings of the Navy, who were finding it intolerable to blockade the French Ports month after month, or else to chase the French ships from the Mediterranean to the West Indies, often without firing a shot.

They had grown used to living on the sparse rations of ships' biscuits filled with weevils, and meat which had been preserved in salt for years.

The main thing that mattered was that the French ambition to conquer England should be checked, and Napoleon defeated.

As if Perry were aware of what the Earl was thinking, he said firmly:

"Forget it, at any rate for the moment. You have been concentrating on Bonaparte for so long that you are beginning to look like him!"

The Earl laughed, then listened attentively to Perry's plans for his amusement.

The first was quite simple.

He produced one of the most attractive women the Earl had ever seen, and the moment he looked into her very expressive dark eyes it was easy to let the stringencies of war fade into the background.

Lucille Gratton was the wife of a Peer much older than herself who had a large but impoverished estate in Ireland.

Because she was exceedingly beautiful, and had been acclaimed from the moment she left the Schoolroom, she expected every man she met to fall at her feet.

She had taken several lovers during her husband's frequent visits to the Emerald Isle, but after a few months she had found them boring.

She was looking for a man that was different and rich when Perry introduced her to the Earl.

After being at sea for so many long months without even seeing a woman, Lucille was a revelation, and to Perry's satisfaction the Earl was captivated.

They dined the first night in a party and the next they were alone together in Lady Gratton's house.

It was inevitable that the Earl should walk home as dawn was breaking, thinking with satisfaction that his years at sea had not prevented him from being a good lover.

He had never met a woman who was more passionate, fiery, or insatiable.

She had accepted his invitation to the Castle, and he knew that, with her presence, the party would be everything he wanted as an introduction to his new position.

He had sent his requirements to the Castle by an old Secretary who had served his father.

Perry had helped him prepare a schedule of the bedrooms, pointing out that the people who were paired together must be as near to each other as possible.

"Is this usual?" the Earl asked.

"I can assure you it is arranged in all the best houses," Perry said. "For Heaven's sake, Durwin, you are old enough to know the facts of life!"

They both laughed, but the Earl could not help thinking it was rather strange that an *affaire de coeur* could take place so blatantly that everybody was aware of it.

It was very different from what it had been in his mother's day.

Yet as far as he was concerned, he was prepared to be carried along on the tide since it was part of Lord Barham's instructions.

As he looked at his Visitor's List, however, he was sure there would not be a spy amongst them.

Nevertheless, perhaps something said would point him in the right direction so that he could do what was expected of him.

Perry's choice among the men had been two Peers whom the Earl had met and liked in the past, a Marquis who would inherit a famous Dukedom, and a Baronet who worked in the Admiralty.

That, with Perry and himself, made six men.

Besides Lucille were five Ladies he had not seen, but who, he had been told, were the *crème de la crème* of the Beauties who embellished Carlton House.

The Earl was certain that everything at the Castle would be as comfortable as he wanted it to be.

He had been glad to hear that some of the old servants were still there.

Bates, the Butler, whom he could remember when he was a small boy; and Mrs. Davison, who used to smuggle chocolate cake and sweets to his room when he had been punished.

There were also one or two other servants who had not died or moved to a better position elsewhere.

As soon as he arrived in England he had appointed a new Estate Manager to the Castle, having learnt that there was no-one in charge.

The man, called Marlow, had been highly recommended by an Admiral with whom he had travelled to London from Portsmouth.

He had sent for him as soon as he arrived in Berkeley Square, and thinking that he seemed efficient, had sent him to the Castle with instructions to discover what needed doing.

It was satisfactory to find that, as his father had been so ill the last years of his life, expenditure had been low.

There was therefore a considerable sum of money in the Bank which he could spend on improvements.

"The first thing I must do," he told himself on receiving a report from his new Manager, "is to visit the Farmers. I am sure I will remember some of them, and of course make sure the Pensioners have been well looked after."

He had a feeling, as he and Perry journeyed to the Castle in a new Phaeton with a team of new horses bought the previous day, that, until the house-party was over, he would have little time for anything else.

There was also an enormous amount to do in Berkeley Square.

The house had been closed up during his father's illness and the servants had either been dismissed or pensioned off.

There was in fact only one man—the Butler—whom he could still remember.

The Earl was used to command and had on several occasions in his life had to recommission a ship in record time.

Compared to that, the house was comparatively easy.

He had also, which was most important, had to buy himself an entire new wardrobe.

He had never had many civilian clothes, and those he had were worn out or he had grown out of them while he was at sea.

Within forty-eight hours of arriving in London he looked respectable enough to venture out of the house.

This was made possible by telling Weston, the fashionable tailor, that he wanted an entire wardrobe and borrowing clothes from him in the meantime.

The fourth day after his return he had visited the Admiralty.

He thought as he tooled his new team of horses with an expertise he had not forgotten, that this actually was the first moment he had been able to relax since he set foot in England.

"I am glad you like Lucille," Perry was saying. "I have always thought her the most beautiful amongst her contemporaries, and far more intelligent than the majority of them."

The Earl tried to remember if he had in fact had an intelligent conversation with Lucille.

He knew if he was truthful that what conversation there had been was on one subject, and one subject only.

He therefore did not reply, and Perry gave him a swift glance, a knowing smile on his lips.

He then began to explain to his friend the history of everybody who was to be in the party, and after they had travelled for nearly two miles the Earl exclaimed:

"Does no-one in London ever give a thought to the war?"

"Not if they can help it!" Perry answered truthfully. "Damn it all, it has gone on too long and we can only pray that by some miracle we shall defeat Napoleon sooner than is expected."

The Earl thought that was improbable.

He told himself it was unlikely that he could ever contribute to Bonaparte's defeat in the way that Lord Barham was expecting.

Therefore, sooner or later he must find something better to do than sleep with beautiful women, and enjoy himself with friends like Perry.

He did not, however, say this aloud.

He had to act the part of a carefree man whose only aim in life was to seek amusement.

It was certainly a thrill when he saw the Castle ahead of him.

It was extraordinary that he was now the possessor of it in his father's place.

It had never crossed his mind while he was at sea that George would be killed and he could be the 11th Earl instead of his brother.

Now he was determined not to let the family down.

George had been groomed for the part since he was a small boy, while Durwin had to take second place and be of little consequence in the family hierarchy.

He remembered once asking his father for a little more money just before he was appointed to a new ship in the rank of Lieutenant.

But his father had explained to him very seriously that anything that could be spared must be given to George.

"He will take my place as the Head of the family," the old Earl had said, "and if his inheritance is frittered away extravagantly, he will be unable to grace

the position as he should, or look after those who
depend upon him."

It had been hard to understand at the time, but
now the Earl knew that, as Head of the Arrow family, there would be innumerable calls on his time and
his purse.

He knew he must be just and not pay one relative
more than another.

As he might have expected, the hostesses he had
met this last week before he left London had all
asked him archly when he intended to get married.

"Not for a very long time," he had replied to Lady
Holland.

She was the only one who said:

"Quite right. Take your time, and when you do
find a woman you love, make sure she will not only
embellish your bed, your table, and the family
jewels, but be a good mother to your children."

It was refreshingly different from what the other
hostesses who had marriageable daughters had told
him.

They thought all that mattered was that the Countess of Arrow should be blue-blooded.

The young girls he had seen so far appeared both
shy and gauche, and it was easy to say firmly that he
had no intention of marrying and could not consider
it until the war was at an end.

It was, of course, Perry who advised him to be
careful of the most ambitious mothers.

"Do not forget, Durwin," he said, "you are more
of a catch these days than you were as a sailor with
no prospects!"

The Earl had laughed.

"I promise you I will not be caught however persuasive the bait may be!"

"Do not boast!" Perry warned him. "Better men than you have been marched up the aisle before they realised what was happening to them!"

"I am not a fool," the Earl said, "and when I do marry, I have no intention of being forced to listen to banal conversation from breakfast until dinner from a woman whose only asset is that her father wears a coronet!"

Perry laughed.

"What is so attractive about you now is that you wear one yourself."

"If you talk like that," the Earl threatened, "I shall return to sea to-morrow! I find the French less terrifying than some of the Dowagers I have met this week!"

As they drew nearer to the Castle, the Earl was thinking how much, as a small boy, he had enjoyed playing in the ancient tower and running through the great State Rooms.

One day he must have a son who would ride the rocking-horse in the Nursery and later have a pony kept for him in the stables until he was old enough to mount a horse.

He would never forget the thrill of jumping a hedge for the first time.

He could remember as vividly as if it were yesterday catching his first trout in the stream near the lake.

"I must say, Durwin," Perry exclaimed, "the Castle certainly looks magnificent! I quite expect to see a number of Knights in chain mail pouring out of the front-door at any moment!"

"I shall be annoyed if there are not a few well-dressed footmen doing that!" the Earl exclaimed.

Because Bates could always be relied on, he was not disappointed.

There was an open bottle of champagne in the ice-cooler in the Study, and *pâté* sandwiches in case they felt hungry after their journey.

"We were late leaving so we had luncheon on the way," the Earl told Bates.

"I thought you might, M'Lord, but the food at the Posting Inns is not very appetising."

"You are quite right," the Earl agreed, "and in future I will take my own food with me."

"That's certainly wise, M'Lord," Bates replied, "and it's what His Lordship your father always did."

As he went to the Study the Earl laughed.

"With Bates to bully me it will be difficult for me to do anything different from what my father always did, the Earl before him, and the Earl before him! In fact, the whole series of them back to the first!"

"And a good thing too!" Perry said. "Far too many of the ancient customs and traditions have been pushed aside. People blame the war, but I actually think it is because they have become sloppy and in-competent."

That at least was something the Earl had never been.

He told himself he would run the Castle as he ran the ship, with an efficiency and a punctiliousness with which no-one could find fault.

He took Perry over the Castle, not only because

he wanted to show it to his friend, but also because he wanted to see it for himself.

He had forgotten how magnificent the State Rooms were.

The Holland covers had been removed from the furniture, and the windows polished until they shone like diamonds.

They were as magnificent as they had been when the Earl was a small boy.

He showed Perry the Long Gallery, the Ball-Room, the Chapel, and the bedrooms, which were mostly named after the Kings and Queens who had slept in them.

When they returned to the Study, Perry threw himself down in a chair and said:

"Well, all I can say is, Durwin, that you are a damned lucky chap!"

"There is still a lot to be done," the Earl replied, "and I must instruct Marlow to find me painters and carpenters as quickly as possible."

"It looks perfect to me as it is," Perry said, "but what about the stables?"

"There I shall certainly need your help," the Earl replied. "Let me see—we bought a dozen horses at Tattersalls and they should have arrived here by now. But I shall want a great many more."

"I suppose you have remembered that you have a house at Newmarket?"

"I had forgotten it until the Prince reminded me. I shall certainly need race-horses, and I want the best!"

"Of course—what else?" Perry laughed mockingly.

The Earl did not reply.

He walked to the window of the Study and was thinking as he looked out into the garden how lucky, how incredibly lucky he was.

But before he bought race-horses, he had every intention of seeing that his estate was looked after and the repairs that were long overdue were put in hand.

He had seen the preliminary list Marlow had made out.

He was horrified to read of the dilapidation of the Alms Houses and the pensioners' cottages, the lack of a School, and, more important, the unemployment of men who had returned from the war.

"There is a lot to do," he told himself.

Actually it lifted his heart to know that he was not going to be idle now that he was no longer at sea.

There was quite a long silence before the door opened and Bates announced:

"The first of Your Lordship's guests have just arrived, and I've shown them M'Lord, into the Blue Drawing-Room."

"Who is here?" Perry asked before the Earl could speak.

"Lady Evelyn Ashby, and Lady Gratton, with two gentlemen, Sir."

Perry looked at the Earl.

"Lucille!" he exclaimed with a knowing note in his voice.

The Earl did not bother to reply, he was moving quickly from the Study, eager to reach the Drawing-Room and Lucille.

* * *

Upstairs, Shenda had been intrigued by the fuss and commotion which had galvanized the whole Castle because the Earl was having a party.

"It'll be like the old times," Mrs. Davison said over and over again.

She showed Shenda the list of the rooms the guests were to occupy.

"There's Lady Evelyn Ashby in the *Charles II Room*," she explained, "another Lady in the *Queen Anne Room*, a third occupies a room called the *Duchess of Northumberland's Room*, and finally, Lady Gratton will occupy the *Queen Elizabeth Room*. That's the Lady his Lordship fancies!"

"How do you know that?" Shenda asked.

Mrs. Davison smiled.

"My niece was fortunate enough to be engaged at Arrow House in Berkeley Square some years earlier, when the old Earl was alive. She loved being there and was real sad when the house was closed."

Shenda nodded to show she understood, and Mrs. Davison went on:

"When she hears His Lordship's back from the sea, she asks if there's a vacancy, and because she comes from the village she were taken on right away!"

"That was lucky for her," Shenda said.

"She wrote to me at once, and I got the letter yesterday, telling me how charming His Lordship is, and as how who she describes as 'the most beautiful Lady in England' is already in his arms, so to speak!"

60

"Do you think he is going to marry her?" Shenda asked.

"Oh, no, Miss Shenda!" Mrs. Davison answered. "Nothing like that! Lady Gratton is married, according to my niece, to a Gentleman as is with his Regiment abroad."

Shenda looked puzzled, and Mrs. Davison, realising she had made a mistake, said quickly:

"The ladies in London have a good time even if their husbands are away from home. There's no use 'wearing your heart on your sleeve' as my mother used to say."

"Yes . . . of course," Shenda agreed.

At the same time, she wondered if she had a husband whether she would feel like going to parties alone and being entertained in the country by Earls.

"There must be many things these ladies would do to help the troops and the seamen," she argued to herself.

Then she thought it was a great mistake to be critical.

She was so lucky to be at the Castle, and although they seemed so far from the war, she had not forgotten the men in the village who were wounded.

Or those families who had sons serving either in the Army or the Navy.

She remembered how sympathetic her father had always been, and when her mother had gone to the village the women used to cry because they had not heard of them for months on end.

Or, if a ship had been sunk, it would be a very

long time before they knew if there were any survivors.

"I wonder if the Earl misses being at sea?" she asked as she went back to her room.

She sat down to continue mending the lace on a sheet which had been torn when it was washed.

As she did so she thought of the extraordinary stories of the Earl's bravery and courage which had reached the village just before he came to the Castle.

Whenever the women went shopping in the Butcher's, the Baker's, the Grocer's or anywhere else, they would congregate round the counter and talk about the war and the latest tales they had heard.

Sooner or later Shenda had heard them too, mostly from Martha when she came in the morning, and from anyone else she met during the day.

"You'll never believe it, Miss Lynd . . ." they would begin.

Then she knew that although Arrowhead seemed a very long way from France, the stories of what was occurring lost nothing in the telling.

Everybody vied with each other to have something new to relate.

She could not remember ever seeing the Earl, although she felt she must have done so when she was a child.

She imagined he would be tall and handsome, like most of the Bows.

There were enough pictures of them in the Castle for her to realise there was a family resemblance going all down the ages.

One of the things that had thrilled her since she had arrived had been the Picture Gallery.

It contained not only portraits, but some very fine works by great artists that had been collected by each successive generation of Arrows since the first.

She was enthralled by the beauty of those which came from Italy, and there was a Fragonard and a Boucher from France that she particularly liked.

There were family portraits on the stairs and along the corridors, and in many of the bedrooms.

It seemed to Shenda that they were watching over the house and the Bow family, and it would have been impossible for the New Earl not to have felt their influence.

In a way it was strange that he should have a large house-party before he had come home and inspected his estate and met those who served him.

He should visit the Farmers who had, she knew, a long list of requests for improvements to their farms.

"He may refuse because of the war," she told herself, "but he can at least repair the roofs and help them build up their stock."

"There are so many things for him to do!" she added as she finished mending the lace.

In fact, she had done it so skillfully that it was impossible to see where it had been torn.

Then with a sigh she told herself it was none of her business and what was most important was that the Earl should not be aware that she was employed in the Castle.

She had a feeling that he would disapprove of a Vicar's daughter being one of his servants.

She felt a little shiver as she thought of how terrible it would be if she had to go away and try to find somewhere else to live.

"We are so happy here," she told Rufus.

She decided she would keep well out of sight until the Earl returned to London and she could have the woods and the garden to herself again.

Rufus was restless and looking at the clock, and she thought she should take him out for a walk before there was any chance of the Earl arriving.

She knew that Bates was expecting His Lordship early in the afternoon.

She therefore hurried down a side staircase with Rufus at her heels and opened the door which led directly into the garden.

Ever since it had been known that the Earl was back from the sea the gardeners had been working overtime to make everything even more beautiful than it had been before.

Because the weather had been warm, the blossom on the trees and shrubs was out.

Spring flowers filled the flower-beds and the grass was as green as a billiard-table.

Shenda took a secret path behind the box-hedges which led up to the Cascade.

It was the place she loved more than anywhere else, and she would watch the water which came from the wood tumbling over the rocks.

There were rock-plants, pink, yellow, and white, to add colour to the grey stones and make it look even more beautiful.

The stone bowl at the bottom of the Cascade was now refilled with goldfish, and they were swimming lazily in and out of the water-lily leaves.

There were buds on the flowers, and she knew they would soon be in bloom.

"It is lovely, lovely, lovely!" Shenda said aloud.

Then, because she was frightened that she might be sent away, she prayed that the Earl would not discover her.

As she did so, she found herself thinking of the Gentleman who had saved Rufus from the trap in the woods.

He had kissed her, and even now she found it difficult to believe it had really happened.

How could she have let a total stranger kiss her on the lips?

She could explain it away only by saying that she had been so bemused by Rufus being in such a predicament, and by the stranger because he looked so different from anybody she had ever seen before.

"It was wrong, but rather wonderful!" she whispered to herself.

Then, because time was passing, and she was afraid she might be seen, she hurried back to the Castle.

"His Lordship's guests have arrived!" Mrs. Davison said, bustling into the room where Shenda was once again sewing.

"Do they look very beautiful?" she asked.

"They certainly does!" Mrs. Davison answered. "And dressed in the height of fashion! If the crowns of their bonnets was any higher, they'd touch the sky!"

Shenda laughed.

Since she had come to the Castle she had found that Mrs. Davison pored over the *Ladies Magazines*, and she had found them not only interesting, but also amusing.

The caricatures done of the Fashionable World were so funny that she wondered if the Ladies and Gentlemen Rowlandson and Cruikshank depicted, and, of course, the Prince of Wales, minded being made to look foolish.

The caricaturists made the Society women grotesquely fat, or else as slim as lathes, and they poked fun at the fashionable transparent gowns and huge, over-decorated bonnets.

They were also very insulting to those who gave themselves airs.

"It's a shame, that's what it is," Mrs. Davison exclaimed, "but all the same, one has to laugh!"

Because she thought it would amuse Shenda, she showed her where in the Library were some actual prints by the caricaturists.

"His late Lordship ordered them first years ago," Mrs. Davison told her. "As soon as they appeared in the shop in St. James's Street, a copy would be sent here."

"He must have enjoyed having them," Shenda remarked.

"He did indeed," Mrs. Davison replied, "and when His Lordship was ill they kept coming because nobody cancelled the order, so they're right up to date, so to speak."

The cartoons told Shenda a great deal about what was known as the Beau Ton and even though she knew they were a cruel exaggeration, she felt she had something to learn from them.

There was a lot to learn too from the books in the Library, which were a joy and a delight to her.

She had packed up every one of her father's

books, determined to keep them, whatever happened.

The Library in the Castle was not only enormous, but until last year, when he became too ill to carry on, there had been a Curator.

He had bought, as he had been instructed to do, books of interest as soon as they were published.

To Shenda it was like being given the keys to Heaven, and she would take half-a-dozen books at a time up to her room.

When she had finished what work she had to do, she would read and read.

She found herself in a new world, and one which she realised carried on her education where it had ended with her father's death.

When she had been young she had been taught by the School-Master, an old Governess who had retired into one of the cottages in the village, and her father.

She wanted to learn, and she thought there was so much to know that there were not enough hours in the day in which to absorb it all.

It was all part of the dream-world she entered when she was in the wood.

Every book she read at the Castle so far had made her realise how much more there was to explore and discover.

"One thing's going to mean more work!" Mrs. Davison was saying.

"What is that?" Shenda asked.

"Lady Gratton's come without her lady's-maid! She had an accident, so they tells me, just before Her Ladyship was ready to leave London."

She sighed.

"That'll leave me short-handed because Rosie'll have to attend to Her Ladyship, and if I knows anything about these 'Ladies of Quality,' it is that they want attention twenty-four hours a day!"

Because she was annoyed, Mrs. Davison almost flounced out of the room, leaving Shenda alone.

She looked after the Housekeeper a little ruefully.

She knew it would be a mistake for her to try to see the beautiful women who were the Earl's guests.

She must keep out of sight, and they were something she would never see, any more than she would see the Earl.

"I must be very, very careful!" she admonished herself.

She spoke aloud, and at the sound of her voice Rufus got up from the chair beside her to put one of his paws on her knee.

"I must be very careful!" she said to him. "And so must you! If you bark and His Lordship hears it, he may say he does not want strange dogs in his house! You might be banished to the stables!"

Because it was something she could not bear to think of, she picked the little dog up in her arms and held him close to her.

"Also," she went on, "we might be sent away, and that must not happen!"

She kissed the top of his head.

"I love it here," she said softly. "You are well fed and so am I, so we must both be very good and very, very careful!"

chapter four

THE Earl, looking down the table in the Great Dining-Room, felt this was a picture he could remember peeping at from the Minstrel's Gallery when he was a small boy.

He used to slip up the small staircase and peep through the carved oak screen at the dinner-parties given by his mother and father.

He always thought his father, sitting at the head of the table in a chair carved with the family arms, looked like a King.

His mother, in a glittering tiara with diamonds at her throat, had come earlier to his bedroom to kiss him good-night.

"You look like a Fairy Princess, Mama!" he told her once, and she had laughed.

She would hold him close in her arms, and he thought when she died that he would always remember her softness and sweetness, and no other woman could ever be like her.

At the moment he was thinking that Lucille and his other lady-guests were, without exception, the most beautiful women gathered together he could ever imagine.

With fair, dark, or fiery red hair, each one of them had a captivating beauty which would be hard for a man to resist.

Especially, he thought with a twist of his lips, one who had been at sea for so long.

When the Armistice had come in 1802, he had not returned to England as so many other Naval Commanders were able to do.

First, because his ship was ordered to remain somewhere in the Mediterranean.

Secondly, because if he did get leave he wanted to see a part of the world that had not been conquered and spoilt by Napoleon.

He had therefore visited Egypt and Constantinople and found a great deal to interest him in Greece.

The countries and their peoples seemed to open up new horizons in his mind, and he had not regretted being away from home for so long.

When he did expect there would be a chance to return, it was too late. Napoleon declared war and Nelson needed him.

It was difficult to believe as course followed course, and the wines from his father's cellars were being poured out on Bates's instructions, that there was a war going on.

The conversation from the spectacular and sophisticated women, as the Earl expected, managed to have a *double entendre* in most of what was said.

Their eyes and lips said a great deal more than was put into words.

"What are we going to do to-morrow?" Lucille Gratton, who was seated on his right, asked.

She had already made it clear what they were doing to-night.

"I have a lot to show you on my estate," the Earl answered, "and a great deal to see for myself. There used to be a Grecian Temple at the end of the garden, and a Watch Tower at the top of the wood, where I remember my mother sometimes arranged picnics."

"You shall show them to me," Lucille said softly, "and, of course, alone."

The Earl wondered if that would make them too conspicuous.

He also had every intention of visiting the stables with Perry.

That would, of course, be done before the ladies condescended to appear downstairs..

He thought it was something he would suggest after breakfast, a meal which he was sure would be attended only by the male members of his party.

When at the end of dinner the ladies left the Dining-Room, there was no need for Lucille to say in a whisper:

"Do not be long, darling Durwin. You know I want you to be with me."

It was something the Earl wanted too, and now tables for cards were arranged in an Ante-Room off the Drawing-Room.

It was obvious, however, that most members of the party were wondering how soon they could decently retire, and the Ladies led the way.

The gentlemen lingered downstairs for a last nightcap, and it was then that Perry said to the Earl:

"You are, as I expected, an excellent host. I have never enjoyed a better dinner!"

"Nor have I!" another guest joined in.

"I shall have some surprises for you to-morrow," the Earl replied, "but you will have to thank Perry for them more than me."

Perry smiled.

"I can only say—give me the right ingredients, and I will provide a good meal!"

They laughed at this and went up to bed, joking together until the Earl said good-night and went into the Master Suite.

When he was undressed and his valet had left him, he knew it was only a step from his room into the *Queen Elizabeth Bedroom* next door.

Lucille was waiting for him.

She flung out her arms and threw back her head to lift her lips to his.

The Earl had the strange feeling that she was like a tigress grasping hungrily at her prey.

* * *

"He's a hero, that's what he is!" Mrs. Davison said. "And if the nation knew all that His Lordship has been adoing, there'd be a statue erected to him as sure as eggs is eggs!"

Mrs. Davison had been relating to Shenda the stories the Earl's valet had been telling them downstairs of his exploits against the French.

There was one which Shenda found particularly fascinating.

English ships had blockaded a dozen French ships of the line in harbour.

The Earl had then sailed into the port in a French frigate which he had captured.

Before they had any idea of his presence he had blown up two French first rates.

"His Lordship's valet was saying," Mrs. Davison related, "that the Captain, as he was then, calls for volunteers and tells them there was every chance they wouldn't come back alive. Yet every man in the ship wanted to accompany him!"

"He could not take them all!" Shenda remarked.

"No, he picked a dozen of those who'd been with him the longest and they set off at midnight, when they thought the Frenchies'd be asleep."

"And they blew up two ships of the line!" Shenda exclaimed.

"Two of the biggest!" Mrs. Davison said with relish. "Then before their crews realised what was happening, they sailed off again with only one mast down, and two men injured."

This was one of a number of stories Shenda was to hear.

She could understand that after each one of them had been repeated round the Castle, it was difficult for anybody to talk of anything else.

"I must see him!" she told herself.

At the same time, she was afraid that if he sent her away, refusing to employ what Mrs. Davison called a "Lady in a subservient position," it would break her heart.

"I must be . . . careful," she said as she had told Rufus last night.

It was only when she knew the whole house-party had gone driving after an early luncheon that she ventured into the garden.

Even then she kept to the shrubbery which led her to the wood before she told Rufus he could run about and exercise his legs.

The woods at the back of the Castle were not as magic to her as the "Knights' Wood" near the Vicarage.

But there was still a magic about them which made Shenda lose herself once more in her dreams.

Only when they had been away from the Castle for nearly two hours did she hurry back just in case some of the house-party returned early from wherever it was they had gone.

She suspected, and later found she was right, that they had driven on what was a delightful track across the Park.

It led through the woods, then up onto a high piece of land on which stood the Watch Tower.

It had been erected by Sir Justin Bow who, having built his Castle, still wanted a place from which he could see the sea.

History related there were guards on duty watching the Danes, in case they again invaded his land.

Shenda had often been in the Watch Tower, and she thought that either Sir Justin had very good eyes or some kind of telescope, even in those early times.

Only on the clearest of days could one see the sea like a streak of light in the far distance.

The Watch Tower itself was unique, although she

imagined the beautiful ladies in their elegant gowns would find it difficult to climb the twisting stone steps which led to the top of the Tower without getting dirty.

'I expect the gentlemen will be only too willing to help them,' she thought with a little smile. 'Or else they will sit in the Guard Room below, where it was always believed Sir Justin kept a number of archers ready to go into battle at a moment's notice.'

She and Rufus reached the Castle, and went in through the Garden Door and up a staircase which was seldom used.

She had been in her Sewing-Room for only two or three minutes when Mrs. Davison came bustling in.

"Oh, there you are, Miss Shenda!" she said. "I've got a job for you."

"What is it?" Shenda asked.

Mrs. Davison held out a pretty reticule which was made of satin and trimmed with tiny rows of lace.

"This belongs to Lady Gratton," she said, "and that stupid Rosie, believe it or not, 'as caught the lace on the corner of the drawer when she was putting it away."

Shenda took the reticule from her.

"It is only a small tear," she said, "and I will mend it so that Her Ladyship will have no idea that such a thing has ever happened!"

"It's always the same with these maids!" Mrs. Davison said crossly. "They're always in far too much of a hurry, wanting to get downstairs and talk to the men, that's what's at the bottom of it!"

"Accidents happen to everybody, so tell Rosie not to be upset," Shenda said. "And bring me anything else that needs mending because I have nothing to do at the moment."

"Well then, you can get on with that gown you're making for yourself," Mrs. Davison said. "I provided you with the material, and the sooner I see you in it, the better!"

"Actually, it is finished!" Shenda said.

"There! What do you think of that!" Mrs. Davison said. "I don't believe old Maggie could have made a dress quicker!"

"I will put it on to-night, and show you," Shenda said. "Actually, I am very proud of it!"

"I've got some more stuff ready for another one," Mrs. Davison answered.

"You are too kind," Shenda said, "and I will pay you for it when I get my first wages."

"You'll do nothing of the sort!" Mrs. Davison said. "And anyway, it's not my material. It's what's been rotting away in the cupboard for years! I can't now remember what we bought it for. I expect her Ladyship had some idea of how she wished to use it."

She glanced at the clock as she finished speaking and gave an exclamation.

"His Lordship's party'll be coming back for tea," she said. "And I've not yet finished inspecting the bedrooms. I can't trust these young maids to leave everything perfect, and that's a fact!"

As she hurried from the room Shenda gave a little laugh.

She knew that Mrs. Davison, after years of only having three old maids under her who she knew worked as well as she did, enjoyed ordering about the new maids who had just come from the village.

They were thrilled at being at the Castle.

When Mrs. Davison bullied them they accepted it as part of their position which considerably enhanced their importance amongst the villagers.

Sitting down at the table which was in the window, Shenda inspected the damaged reticule.

She had learnt that Lady Gratton had worn a gown of emerald green gauze at dinner last night.

The slip beneath it was so transparent that Mrs. Davison had said she might as well have been naked.

Because she had given her extra work, Mrs. Davison did not admire Lady Gratton as much as she did two of the other ladies.

Also, although she did not say so, Shenda guessed she thought that however beautiful she was, she was not good enough for the Earl.

He had now assumed a kind of God-like position in Mrs. Davison's mind.

She thought the only woman who would be good enough for him, or would be his equal, would be a Queen, or at least a goddess!

The reticule was made of green satin which was the same colour as the gown about which Mrs. Davison had been so scathing.

The narrow lace that ran round it in rows was, she knew, hand-made, and must have been very expensive.

She found some silk thread in her work-basket that matched it.

Opening the top of the reticule which was pulled together by a ribbon which a Lady could hold over her arm, Shenda was aware that there were some things inside it.

She carefully took them out.

There was a handkerchief edged with lace and exquisitely embroidered with Lady Gratton's initials.

There was a tiny gold box containing lip-salve, and another larger box which was rather like a snuff-box, which Her Ladyship used for powder.

Shenda looked at them with interest, thinking they were a very luxurious way of carrying cosmetics.

She found one box had a clasp set with diamonds, while the other had the initial "L" on it in sapphires.

"I suppose they were presents from her husband," she told herself.

Then, as she put her hand under the framework to hold it firm so as to mend the lace on the outside, she thought there was something else in the bag.

It was only a small piece of paper, and she drew it out in case she should tear it by mistake.

It was folded over, and when she opened it out she saw to her surprise there were a number of words in French written in a small, strong hand-writing.

Forgetting it was perhaps private, she read:

Où se trouve le groupe de l'Expédition Secrète? £500
Pour découvrir l'emplacement de Nelson £100.

Shenda read it and read it again, and told herself she must be imagining what she saw.

Then she knew unmistakably that what she had inadvertently stumbled upon was a request from a

French spy to Lady Gratton, and she was very intimate with the Earl!

If anybody knew the answers to these questions, then it would be he.

She read the message over and over again before putting the paper on the table under the handkerchief and starting to mend Lady Gratton's reticule.

It did not take her long, and when she had finished it, she put the little boxes and the handkerchief back.

Then she knew with a sudden constriction of her heart that she had to warn the Earl.

She went to a desk that Mrs. Davison had arranged for her in the corner of the room, and picking up her pen, copied exactly and in the same handwriting the words on the piece of paper.

As she returned the piece of paper to the reticule she was frightened because she had to face the Earl.

It was one thing to hide from him because she had no wish to have to leave the Castle.

It was quite another to be in possession of the knowledge that one of his visitors was spying for the French, of which he was not aware.

The difficulty, she knew, would be to see the Earl alone without the household thinking it very strange.

The majority of the servants believed she was only a seamstress.

She thought the matter over for some time, then knew the only person she could trust would be Bates, whom she had known for years.

He, like Mrs. Davison, had been very fond of her mother and father.

When Mrs. Davison came back into the room,

Shenda handed her the reticule. She looked for the tear and exclaimed:

"That's really clever of you, Miss Shenda! I'd defy anybody to find what I can't see with my own eyes!"

"I am glad you are pleased." Shenda smiled.

"Rosie will be!" Mrs. Davison remarked. "I tells her—one more carelessness like that, and she goes back to the village!"

"Oh, Mrs. Davison, you could not be so cruel," Shenda protested. "You know how her mother and the whole family are delighted for her to be here with you, when they were afraid she might have to go to work in London and perhaps get into trouble."

"Well, if I say it myself, I looks after my girls!" Mrs. Davison answered.

"Of course you do," Shenda said, "and Mama always used to say how lucky they were to be under you, and that being in the Castle was the best training any girl could have."

"Well, I does my best," Mrs. Davison said modestly, but she was smiling as, carrying the reticule, she left the room.

Shenda looked at the clock.

She knew by this time the house-party would have returned.

They would have had tea and the ladies would most certainly by now have retired to their bedrooms to rest before dinner.

She therefore slipped down the back stairs, peeped into the Pantry, and was lucky to find Bates there alone, taking the silver ornaments that would be required at dinner out of the safe.

He was very proud of the silver and would trust no-one with it except himself.

At night when it was put away, every piece was wrapped specially in green baize and put in its own place in the safe.

He was just putting a magnificent silver basket designed by Paul Lameric down on the Pantry table.

Then, when he saw Shenda, he exclaimed:

"Look at this, Miss Shenda! I've not been able to use it for three years. It's nice for it to come out of the darkness!"

He spoke as if the basket had feelings like his own, and Shenda replied:

"No-one could have kept it looking as beautiful as you have."

He smiled at her, then, thinking it was rather strange for her to be coming into the Pantry, he asked:

"Be there anything I can do for you, Miss Shenda?"

"Yes, there is," Shenda replied. "I have to see His Lordship alone, and it is very important!"

Bates took off the green baize apron he was wearing and put on his jacket.

"Come with me, Miss," he said. "I think, if I'm not mistaken, His lordship'll be in his Study seeing to the letters which he's had no time to deal with earlier."

They walked along the wide passage that led from the Pantry past the Dining-Room and, passing several other rooms, reached the hall.

There were four footmen on duty who straightened themselves as Bates appeared and looked directly ahead, as they had been taught to do.

On the other side of the hall was another wide passage which led past the Rubens Room and on to the Great Library, which was as large as three ordinary rooms put together.

They reached the Study, and Bates paused for a moment outside it.

Shenda realised he was listening to hear if there were voices coming from inside it.

Then he made a gesture to her to stand back so that if by any chance the Earl was not alone, she would not be seen.

Then he opened the door.

There was a short pause as he looked around the room, then he said:

"Excuse me, M'Lord, but could you spare a moment for somebody who wants to see Your Lordship —and it's important!"

"I suppose so!" the Earl said, looking up from the desk at which he was sitting. "Who is it?"

Bates deliberately avoided the question, only gesturing to Shenda to enter the room.

She came in slowly, holding her head high.

At the same time, she was conscious that she felt nervous because it was the first time she had seen the Earl, although she had heard so much about him.

He was finishing off a letter he had been writing when Bates had interrupted him.

Shenda had almost reached his desk before he raised his head.

Then, as he did so, she gave a little exclamation and without thinking she said:

"Oh—it is you!"

Sitting looking at her was the Gentleman who had rescued Rufus, and who before he had left her had kissed her for the first time in her life.

She was astonished to see him, having been told over and over again that this was the first time the Earl had come to the Castle.

It had therefore never struck her for one moment that the stranger who had lifted her onto the saddle of his horse could be the Earl.

Now they were both staring at each other, and as he recovered first from his surprise he asked:

"Why are you here?"

He rose slowly to his feet as he spoke.

Then, as if they both found it hard to say any more, they stood looking at each other until Shenda said in a small voice he could hardly hear:

"I . . . I had to . . . see you . . . and it is very . . . important!"

"You did not know who I was?" he asked.

"I . . . I had no . . . idea!"

It seemed as if it were an effort as the Earl said:

"As you wanted to see me, I suggest you sit down and tell me why you have come to the Castle."

He walked round the desk and indicated a sofa that stood on one side of the fireplace.

As he did so he saw that Shenda was not wearing a bonnet and looked exactly as she had when he had found her in the wood.

Since she had sat down on the sofa she had not looked at him, and he realised she was shy.

To put her at ease, he asked:

"I trust Rufus has recovered from his ordeal in the wood?"

"Y-yes . . . he is quite . . . all right," Shenda replied, "but . . . I realise now that it was . . . your trap that I asked you to . . . throw away!"

"It was put there on my Estate Manager's instructions," the Earl explained, "but I have now given him orders that there are to be no traps in Knights' Wood, or any other wood around the Castle."

"Oh . . . thank . . . you," Shenda cried. "That is . . . kind and . . . very wonderful of you. I have been . . . worried in case . . . Rufus should be caught in another one."

"I promise you he is quite safe," the Earl replied.

He saw the gratitude in her eyes.

Then, as if he forced himself to speak sensibly, he said:

"Now, tell me, if you did not know who I was, why did you want to see the owner of the Castle."

Shenda drew in her breath.

Somehow it was even harder now that she knew who he was to tell him about what she had found.

Then she told herself that anyone who was endangering the lives of British soldiers and sailors must be dealt with and quickly.

Without speaking she held out to the Earl the piece of paper on which she had copied what had been written in Lady Gratton's reticule.

He took it from her, looking at her face as he did so, thinking she was even more lovely than he remembered.

Then he looked down at the paper and stiffened.

He read it, then he asked in a very different tone:

"Where did you get this?"

"I . . . copied it from a piece of paper I . . . f-found in a lady's reticule," Shenda replied.

"A lady's reticule?" the Earl enquired. "Where did you handle such a thing?"

"Here in . . . the Castle," Shenda murmured.

"But why? What were you doing here?"

There was a distinct pause before Shenda answered in a hesitating little voice:

"I . . . I am your new . . . Seamstress, My Lord."

The Earl stared at her has if he could hardly believe what he had heard. Then his said:

"Who engaged you, and why?"

"The . . . old Seamstress died three years ago . . . and Mrs. Davison did not . . . appoint anybody else . . . until she knew Your Lordship . . . returned."

"So you have just come here?"

"Yes . . . My Lord."

"And you handled this lady's reticule! What lady?"

Shenda drew in her breath.

"Lady . . . Gratton!"

The Earl's lips tightened, then he said:

"I do not believe it! How is it possible?"

He was, Shenda realised, speaking to himself rather than to her, and after a moment she said:

"I . . . thought it only . . . right, My Lord . . . that I should bring it . . . to you."

"You can understand it although it is written in French?"

"I . . . I speak . . . French, My Lord."

"Have you any idea what it refers to?"

"Yes."

"What do you mean—yes?"

There was a little pause before Shenda answered:

"I . . . have . . . heard of . . . the Secret Expedition."

The Earl stared at her as if he could not believe what he had heard.

"You have heard of the Secret Expedition?" he asked, and his voice was very sharp. "Who could have told you?"

He sounded to Shenda so astonished that she could not help smiling.

"The Doctor's son . . . My Lord . . . is one of the . . . Officers being carried with the . . . members of his Regiment . . . among the . . . transports which . . . make up the Expedition."

The Earl put his hand up to his forehead.

"I think I must be dreaming! The whole thing is meant to be a secret!"

"I know that," Shenda said, "but when Lieutenant Doughty came home he told his father what he had been . . . chosen to do . . . and the Doctor told my . . . father."

"Are you telling me that the whole village is now aware and talking of the Expedition?"

"Oh . . . no . . . My Lord. Guy Doughty swore his father to secrecy . . . and my father never . . . repeated anything that was . . . told to him . . . confidentially."

"I suppose I should be relieved about that!" the Earl said sarcastically. "Well, what do you make of it, and I suppose you do not know the answer . . ."

"I think I do, My Lord," Shenda replied.

The Earl stared as if he were past finding words for what he was feeling.

"One of the seamen in . . . Admiral Nelson's . . . ship," Shenda said, "is married to one of the . . .

village girls who has returned to . . . live with her parents until . . . he returns from the . . . fighting. Knowing they had to be very careful . . . he writes to her in a special code."

"And he told her where Admiral Nelson is?" the Earl asked incredulously.

As if she could not help being amused at his bewilderment, Shenda's eyes twinkled.

He could see the suspicion of a dimple on one side of her mouth as she said:

"In his last letter he wrote:

> *My left hand's itching, and I shall be*
> *thinking to-morrow of the cake that your*
> *mother always bakes on a Sunday.*"

The Earl was speechless, waiting for Shenda to explain.

"Because . . . he loves her . . . wherever he is he . . . stands facing England. If his left hand is itching, it means he is travelling West, and the cake her mother always bakes on Sundays is a Madeira!"

"I do not believe this!" the Earl exclaimed.

He sat down in a chair as he spoke and, holding the paper Shenda had given him in his hand, stared at it.

His brain began to work shrewdly and logically.

If this message, as Shenda had said, had been found in Lucille Gratton's reticule, then it was her pleading eyes and pouting lips about which Lord Barham had warned him.

She was receiving money for the information she

obtained from her lovers, which was of use to the French.

Whoever was communicating with her must have been aware that she was with him.

As he had just come back to England from the Mediterranean, and was in touch with the Admiralty, he was more likely to know than anybody else.

For a moment he was so furious at being deceived that he wanted to confront Lucille Gratton with her perfidy and tell her exactly what he thought of her.

Then he knew that far more important than his feelings was to root out the spy or spies that directed her and were working for Napoleon.

He sat for some minutes, although it seemed longer, without speaking.

Then he said to Shenda:

"I presume Lady Gratton does not realise that you have found this?"

"No, My Lord, the maid who looks after her tore the lace on the reticule and Mrs. Davison gave it to me to mend."

"So she has not seen you?"

"No, My Lord."

"But you are here, working in the Castle, and I presume employed by me!"

"Yes, My Lord."

She wondered what the Earl was thinking.

"I wonder, Shenda, if you are prepared to do something to help your country? I must warn you, however, that it may be dangerous."

Shenda looked at him in surprise. Then she said:

"I will do . . . anything, My Lord . . . to . . . help

men like yourself . . . defeat Napoleon, and end this . . . horrible . . . wicked war!"

"I thought you would feel like that," the Earl said, "and what I am going to ask you to do is to maid Lady Gratton whilst she is staying here."

Shenda's eyes seemed to fill her whole face. She had never imagined that she would be asked to do such a thing.

For a moment she thought it was something she must refuse because she was quite certain her mother would not approve.

Then she asked herself what was more important, that she was a Lady, which the Earl did not think of her as being, or that she should fight, as he had fought, against an enemy which at the moment was holding all the trump cards?

With an effort, because she was a little frightened, she said:

"I will do . . . anything you . . . ask me . . . My Lord."

"Thank you," the Earl answered. "I am going to be frank with you, Shenda, because I think you are intelligent, and will understand when I tell you that what you have brought me is at this moment of inestimable value to the Admiralty!"

"I thought it must be . . . something like . . . that."

"First," the Earl said, "will you promise me that you will not speak of anything you have told me or repeat our conversation here in this room to anybody else in the Castle, or elsewhere?"

"I promise!" Shenda said. "And I have not . . . in fact told anybody except . . . Bates that I even . . . wanted to . . . see you!"

"Good!" the Earl said. "Now I will tell Mrs. Davison that as I want Lady Gratton to be exceptionally comfortable and happy, I would like you to look after her."

"I think, My Lord, that Mrs. Davison is going to think it strange that I have met you."

"I can explain that to her by saying that when I got back to England, I went first to my house in Berkeley Square," the Earl said quickly, "which I found in a terrible mess."

He paused to see if she was listening before he went on:

"I then decided to see the Castle after all the years I had been away, and find out if it was just as it had always been."

He went on with a faint smile:

"I had not seen it for fourteen years, and I think I was half-afraid it would turn out to be an illusion, and I would find the walls crumbling, the roof caved in, and the way I used to dream of it would be just a mirage."

"I can understand . . . that," Shenda said in a soft voice.

"I got up before dawn," the Earl went on, "and, hiring the best possible horse, I rode here from London just to look at the Castle."

He drew in his breath before he said:

"It was there, and just as I had dreamed of it!"

He saw the understanding in Shenda's eyes which he thought were very lovely as he went on:

"I had no intention of meeting anybody, knowing

it would be a mistake to appear unannounced and unexpected."

He smiled at her.

"Then you know what happened! I found a very lovely person in the wood and was of service to her."

"You were . . . very kind," Shenda murmured, "and I shall never forget how you . . . helped Rufus . . . but I had no idea . . . it never crossed my . . . mind that you were the . . . new Earl!"

"I went straight back to London, and found it difficult to believe that you were real," the Earl said, "or that there was a magic wood in which I found you."

The way he spoke made Shenda blush, and she looked away from him.

"Now we meet again," the Earl said as if he forced himself to speak naturally, "and if you needed my help, I now need yours! Napoleon's spies. I am told, are everywhere, but I can hardly believe it possible that they are actually in my own home!"

There was a hint of fury in his voice that Shenda did not miss as he went on:

"Now, as I have said, you and I have to find the spy behind the spy; the man who gives the orders, the man or woman who is in touch with Bonaparte."

"I am . . . sure it will be . . . very difficult," Shenda murmured.

"I have yet to lose a battle," the Earl replied, "and with your help, Shenda, I will win this one!"

He rose to his feet as he spoke, and as she did the same they looked at each other, then he took her hand in his.

For a moment his eyes were on her lips.

Then, as she suddenly felt very shy, he lifted her hand and kissed it.

"Thank you, Shenda!" he said. "And be careful! These people are dangerous!"

chapter five

WHEN Shenda left the Earl she ran upstairs to find Mrs. Davison.

She was not in her room so Shenda searched for her and finally found her in the Linen Cupboard.

Just as she arrived a footman in front of her was saying:

"His Lordship wishes to see you, Mrs. Davison, in th' Study."

"I'll come at once," Mrs. Davison said, putting down the pillow-cases she was sorting.

She would have followed the footman, but Shenda caught hold of her arm.

"Listen," she said in a whisper, "I have just . . . seen His Lordship, and whatever he . . . asks you to do . . . regarding me . . . agree, but do not . . . tell him who . . . I am."

Mrs. Davison looked at her in surprise, then rea-

93

lising his Lordship was waiting, hurried after the footman.

Shenda went to her room and sat down, holding her hands over her eyes.

How could she have imagined that this would happen? That her whole position in the Castle would be in jeopardy because of Lady Gratton?

Then she knew that whatever the cost to herself, there was nothing more important than that Napoleon's spies should not be successful in obtaining the information they sought.

* * *

In the Study the Earl said:

"Come in, Mrs. Davison, I want to speak to you."

Mrs. Davison went towards the desk where he was sitting, and curtsied.

"I hopes everything's to your satisfaction, My Lord."

"You have done marvels in such a short time," the Earl replied, "and I am very grateful."

There was a little pause, then he went on:

"I want to speak to you about Lady Gratton."

"Lady Gratton, M'Lord?" Mrs. Davison exclaimed.

"She is very fastidious," the Earl said, "and she requires special maiding, as her own lady's-maid has had an accident."

Mrs. Davison stiffened, as if she thought he was complaining, and he went on:

"I thought as you have Shenda in the Castle, who is, I am sure, an excellent seamstress, she might look after Lady Gratton for the last two days she is here."

94

He was watching the effect of his words and did not miss the expression of consternation on his Housekeeper's face.

She parted both lips as if she were about to protest at what he was asking.

However, with an effort she said meekly:

"Very well, M'Lord, if that's your wish, I'll speak to Shenda."

"Thank you, Mrs. Davison," the Earl said.

Feeling it would be a mistake to say any more, he picked up his pen and, realising she was dismissed, Mrs. Davison curtsied and left the room.

Upstairs she went at once to Shenda and asked:

"Now, Miss Shenda, what's all this about, and how's His Lordship aware that you're in the Castle?"

Shenda rose to her feet and drew Mrs. Davison to the sofa which had been arranged in the room when the bed was removed.

"I have known you ever since I was a little girl," she said in her soft voice, "and as you know, Mama was so fond of you, and Papa always said everything at the Castle would be all right so long as you were here."

There was a smile on Mrs. Davison's lips as she went on:

"I am going to ask you now to believe there is a very good reason for me to look after Lady Gratton, so please do not ask any questions which I cannot answer."

"I don't understand," Mrs. Davison protested, "and that's a fact!"

"I know," Shenda said, "and I am sure later I shall be able to explain everything to you, although, of course, to no-one else, why His Lordship has asked me to look after Lady Gratton."

"If you asks me," Mrs. Davison said, "it's something you shouldn't be doing, and I can't understand His Lordship suggesting such a thing even though she does want some of her gowns altered, free of charge, so to speak."

Shenda realised this had been the Earl's explanation, and she said quickly:

"You know, Mrs. Davison, it is a very good thing for me to make myself useful, then His Lordship will not think that I am too young for the position, and that Rufus and I should not be at the Castle."

"Well, there's certainly that to think of!" Mrs. Davison admitted grudgingly.

Shenda kissed her cheek.

"Just make sure if possible that nobody talks about it below stairs," she said, "and when His Lordship goes away I am sure he will forget all about me."

She saw Mrs. Davison was pacified.

At the same time, she could not help thinking that unless she could provide the Earl with further evidence of Lady Gratton's espionage, he would undoubtedly forget her when he returned to London.

She was very conscious of how, when he had kissed her, it had been a strange sensation which it was impossible to forget.

*   *   *

As it happened, the Earl had not forgotten Shenda, and he found himself thinking of her and what she had discovered all the time he was dressing for dinner.

He went downstairs to the Drawing-Room, where his guests who were staying in the house and a number of neighbours were to congregate before dinner.

He thought that whereas before he had admired and desired Lucille, now she only revolted him.

He wondered how he could ever have found her attractive when her hands were stained with the blood of men she was prepared to sell to the enemy for a little more than "thirty pieces of silver."

He thought it would give him the greatest pleasure to expose her and for her to be taken to the Tower of London for interrogation.

Then he knew that if he was to collect the information Lord Barham required, he had to play the most difficult part he had ever played in his whole life.

It was one thing to defeat the enemy in the heat of battle.

It was quite another to pretend a desire he did not feel for a woman whom he regarded as being as dangerous as a rattle-snake.

Yet he knew Lucille must not have the slightest suspicion that his ardency had cooled because he was suspicious of her.

If she did, then the man they wanted, the spy who could hand out Napoleon's gold so liberally, would disappear.

The years of being in the Navy, especially when he was the Captain of a ship, had taught the Earl to have complete control over himself and his emotions.

Just as he would never show fear in the face of overwhelming odds, so he was now determined that for the sake of England Lucille must not learn of his true feelings towards her.

At the same time, when she looked at him with a flame in her eyes, and he listened to words which in the past would have fired his passion, he hated her.

Then, as she attempted to monopolise him at dinner and later when the party gambled at the card-tables and he was expected to pay her debts, he kept thinking of two grey eyes.

They were as clear and innocent as a child's, and he thought of the softness of Shenda's lips when he had kissed her.

He knew he should not have allowed anything so lovely and so perfect to come in contact with Lucille.

He was aware that the voluptuousness of their love-making would shock Shenda.

He could not allow her to suspect the depths of depravity which existed in a sophisticated woman who purported to be a Lady.

Yet if Shenda was to maid Lucille, she would in the morning see the untidy bed and the crumpled pillows.

However pure and innocent she might be, she would have some idea of what had taken place during the night.

It was then the Earl made up his mind that he must protect Shenda as much as possible.

When he was with Lucille in a corner of the Drawing-Room and for the moment out of ear-shot of the other guests, he said in a low voice:

"To-night—come to me."

"To your room?" Lucille asked in surprise.

"I will explain later," he replied, "but do as I ask."

At that moment they were interrupted by one of the guests who wished to leave and he said no more.

When Lucille, in a diaphanous nightgown and enveloped in a seductive French perfume, came into his bedroom, he thought that at least Shenda would not see any evidence of the crime.

*   *   *

A long time later, when they were lying side by side and the Earl knew that Lucille was for the moment satisfied, she said in a very soft tone:

"Do you darling, wonderful Durwin, miss being at sea?"

"Yes, of course," the Earl answered, "it is hard to start an entirely new life when you are as old as I am."

Lucille laughed.

"I do not know a younger man who could be more ardent or more irresistible," she said. "But even when you are loving me, I am wondering if you would rather be sailing over the waves on a secret expedition."

There was a little silence, then the Earl yawned.

"You have made me so sleepy," he said, "that all I can think of at the moment is that I will not have to get up at some unearthly hour for the Dawn Watch!"

Lucille was silent, but he knew she was trying to think of how she could broach the subject again.

After a moment she said:

"Tell me what you think of Admiral Nelson. Is he

really as sexually attractive as he is reputed to be?"

She waited for an answer, thinking that perhaps she could ask the Earl casually if Lord Nelson was at the moment with Lady Hamilton.

Then, to her surprise, as she turned towards him she found that he was asleep.

*   *   *

Shenda found it easier to maid Lady Gratton than she had expected.

When she had started to help Her Ladyship dress for dinner she asked:

"Where is the maid who was looking after me? I think her name was Rosie."

"That is right, M'Lady, but she is slightly indisposed this evening, and the Housekeeper asked me to take her place."

Shenda was wearing the mob-cap which all the maids at the Castle wore.

She had pulled it low on her forehead, and its frill almost obscured her eyes, but Lady Gratton hardly gave her a glance before she said:

"Well, I hope you know what to do. I have no wish to explain things twice."

"No, of course not, M'Lady, and I am the Seamstress in the Castle, so if there is anything Your Ladyship wants altering, I can do it for you."

Lady Gratton was instantly interested.

"I was going to pin the slip under the gown I am wearing to-night, which is slightly too large," she said. "If you get a needle and thread, you can sew me into it, but do not forget you will have to cut me loose when I come to bed."

"No, of course not, M'Lady, and to-morrow I will alter the buttons so that it fits you perfectly."

"That is a good idea," Lady Gratton said, "and I have another gown that needs a slight alteration."

She put out quite a number of dresses before she went down to dinner, and Shenda took them up to the Sewing-Room.

Because she knew she would have to sit up until Lady Gratton came to bed so that she could undress her, she took to her bedroom one of the books she had borrowed from the Library.

She was so immersed in it that it was quite a surprise to find when Lady Gratton came to bed that it was after one o'clock.

Her Ladyship was obviously in a hurry to be undressed, and when she was arrayed in what Shenda thought was the most revealing nightgown she had ever imagined, she said sharply:

"That will be all! You may go now, and call me at ten o'clock to-morrow morning, not before!"

"Very good, M'Lady," Shenda murmured.

"And do not forget the clothes you have to alter for me," Lady Gratton added.

"Of course not, M'Lady."

As Shenda hurried along the passage and up the stairs to her own room, it just passed through her mind that Lady Gratton had not got into bed.

She supposed she had a reason for not doing so.

Then, because she was tired, she undressed and fell asleep as soon as her head touched the pillow.

*   *   *

The next day Shenda helped Lady Gratton to dress and arranged her hair so skillfully that she was delighted.

She had also altered two of the gowns to her satisfaction.

Later, when she was dressing for dinner, Lady Gratton said:

"As I am returning to London to-morrow, I intend to ask His Lordship if he will let you maid me until my own lady's-maid has recovered. There are quite a number of garments at my house in London I would like you to alter and refurbish for me."

Shenda drew in her breath.

She wanted to say that such an idea was impossible, then she knew she must ask the Earl's permission before she could refuse.

Hesitatingly she said:

"If I am . . . allowed to come . . . M'Lady . . . I am afraid I must bring my small dog with me . . . he is very good . . . but he is always . . . with me . . . and it would . . . break his heart if I . . . left him behind."

"A dog?" Lady Gratton exclaimed as if it were some strange animal of which she had never heard. "Well, if you promise me it will be no trouble, and does not come into the front of the house, I suppose I must put up with it!"

"Thank you . . . very much . . . M'Lady."

As soon as Lady Gratton had gone down to luncheon Shenda wrote a little note to the Earl that was very short—just one line saying:

Please, I must see Your Lordship—Shenda.

She went down the back stairs and gave it to Bates, who was in the Pantry, thinking it would be a mistake if anybody saw her in what the servants called "the front of the house."

She would have been very foolish if she had not realised that the gingham gown with which Mrs. Davison had provided her looked very different on her than it did on the other maids.

The mob-cap, however she wore it, seemed to accentuate the shape of her chin, the size of her eyes, and the classical symmetry of her little nose.

Shenda knew that Bates, however surprised he might be at her request, would ask no questions.

"I'll hand it to his Lordship when no-one's about, Miss Shenda," he said.

Shenda smiled at him, then ran upstairs to the safety of her own room

She had the feeling that she was walking on a tight-rope and at any moment might fall into some horrible dark pit from which there was no escape.

She might have guessed, she thought later, that the Earl would respond to her note in an original fashion.

Bates came up to her Sitting-Room carrying in his hand a book describing the history of the Castle.

"His Lordship says, Miss, that he thinks this is the volume you require, and hopes you'll find in it the reference to the village for which you're looking."

"Thank you!" Shenda said. "It is very kind of His Lordship to lend me anything so interesting."

When Bates had gone she opened the book to find as she expected a note so small that she had to turn a number of pages before she discovered it.

It contained just five words:

The Greek Temple — six o' clock.

She calculated that she would just have time to meet the Earl and be back to help prepare Lady Gratton's bath and undress her for dinner.

At a quarter to six she left the Castle by the Garden Door and with Rufus at her heels hurried behind the shrubs, and past the Bowling Green.

Beyond the Cascade there was a Greek Temple which had been brought back to England by the 8th Earl at the beginning of the last century.

It was a very pretty Temple with Ionic pillars at the front and a room behind in which there was a statue of Aphrodite with a dove on her shoulder and another in her hand.

The Earl was waiting there when Shenda arrived.

He thought as she came towards him, silhouetted against the rhododendron bushes, that she might have been Aphrodite herself risen again from the sea to bemuse mankind.

Because it pleased Mrs. Davison, Shenda, when she was not working, discarded the gingham dress.

She now had on a new gown she had made from the embroidered muslin which Mrs. Davison had given her.

She had made it in the fashionable style that all the ladies in the house-party were wearing, with a high waist, and ribbons crossing over the breast with the ends cascading down the back.

The sun, sinking low in the sky, picked out the

gold in her hair, and it seemed to the Earl that she came towards him in a blaze of light.

As Shenda reached him he looked so handsome and so elegant standing against the white pillars that for a moment she forgot to curtsy, and they just stood looking at each other.

Then with an effort the Earl asked:

"You wanted to see me?"

"I had to ask . . . Your Lordship what I . . . should do," Shenda replied, "as Her Ladyship has asked me to go to . . . London with her to-morrow . . . and maid her until her own lady's-maid has . . . recovered from her . . . accident."

The Earl frowned.

"She has not mentioned it to me!"

"I . . . I think she will do so to-night."

The Earl looked away from Shenda back towards the Castle.

He knew with every nerve in his body although he did not like to acknowledge it, that he hated the idea of anyone so young and unsophisticated coming in contact with Lucille.

And yet, he asked himself, what else could he do but allow Shenda to go?

"You have found nothing else?" he asked after a moment.

"Nothing, My Lord."

The Earl sighed.

"Then I suppose I must ask you, Shenda, once again to help me."

"Y-you want me to . . . go to London?"

"It is something I do *not* want," he said harshly, "but it is, I feel, the one chance we have of finding out who is behind this despicable and criminal behaviour on the part of a Lady who is English-born."

"Do you think the man, or whoever it is, will be indiscreet enough to . . . come to Her Ladyship's house?"

"I do not know the answer," the Earl said. "We can only pray, you and I, Shenda, that you may by some lucky chance pick up a clue which will lead us to the man who is spying for Napoleon, and undoubtedly at the instigation of Fouché, the most astute and dangerous man in France."

He looked questioningly at Shenda as he spoke, as if she might not know of whom he was speaking, and she said:

"I think you are referring to the Minister of Police."

"How do you know that?" the Earl asked.

"My father told me about him," Shenda answered, "and of the way he has forced many of the *émigrés* to work for him by threatening to kill their relatives who were still in France."

The Earl looked surprised.

It flashed through his mind that in some way this exquisite creature facing him might become involved with a man who during the revolution used to arrive at the Guillotine with a pair of human ears dangling from either side of his hat.

Then he told himself he was being over-imaginative, and the Channel lay between Shenda and the most cruel and unscrupulous of all Napoleon's servants.

"What I would ask you to do," he said, "is to go to London with Her Ladyship, but stay only as briefly as possible. If she tries to keep you, and you wish to leave, make some excuse that you are required at the Castle, and have to return as arranged."

"I . . . understand," Shenda said in a small voice.

"But if by any chance you think you are in danger," the Earl said quickly, "if you feel that somebody is suspicious of you, or you find the position intolerable, then my house in Berkeley Square is only a short distance from Lady Gratton's."

He thought there was relief in Shenda's very expressive eyes, and he said:

"Go there immediately, and if I am not there, tell my Secretary, Mr. Masters, to find me. I will always inform him where I am so that there will be as little delay as possible."

"I . . . I understand," Shenda said, "but it is rather . . . frightening!"

The Earl took a step nearer to her.

"Are you quite certain you can do this?" he asked. "If you are really afraid, then I promise, I will understand, and you can stay here at the Castle."

She looked up at him, and he liked the way she lifted her chin a little higher, as if to stiffen her own pride.

"If I can save the life of one seaman," she said, "then however uncomfortable and frightening it may be, it is something I must do!"

"Thank you," the Earl said simply.

He was looking at her, and once again his eyes were on her lips. She felt the colour come into her cheeks.

"I . . . I must go back," she said. "Her Ladyship wishes to be woken at six-thirty."

She did not wait for the Earl to reply, but turning, sped away from him as if she had wings on her feet.

As he watched her go, he had an almost uncontrollable impulse to run after her, and take her in his arms.

She was too beautiful to be concerned with danger, or the disgusting degradation of foreign spies, especially when they were women using their looks and bodies in order to obtain the information Bonaparte required.

Then he told himself that whatever the cost, England must come first, and no-one knew better than he that the Secret Expedition must reach its destination safely.

If Shenda had not warned him, he might have inadvertently, he thought, said something which would have betrayed it.

And yet with all the secrecy and warnings, it seemed inconceivable that two people in the quiet little village of Arrowhead should know not only that the Secret Expedition had left England, but that Nelson was on his way to Jamaica.

He knew that his first priority when he arrived in London to-morrow was to take what information he had so far to Lord Barham.

*　　*　　*

Shenda, in her gingham dress and mob-cap, called Lady Gratton at exactly six-thirty.

She was asleep when Shenda entered the room, but roused herself to say drowsily:

"Oh, Heavens! Is it time to get up? I was dreaming."

"What of, Your Ladyship?" Shenda asked.

"That I could afford to purchase the most delecta-

108

ble evening wrap that I saw in Bond Street last week."

"Was it so very beautiful?" Shenda asked.

"It was of ermine, and lined with a silk that exactly matched my eyes!"

"It sounds very becoming, M'Lady."

"If it costs five hundred pounds," Lady Gratton said dreamily, "I am determined it shall be mine!"

Shenda drew in her breath.

She wondered how any woman, whatever nationality, could sacrifice men's lives for a fur she could wear over her white shoulders.

"She is wicked . . . evil!" Shenda told herself.

She wondered as she did so how the Earl could be infatuated with anyone who could be so utterly despicable.

He was so strong, so brave, so exactly what an Englishman should be, and obviously a good judge of men.

But his perception had failed when he encountered a woman who might be beautiful, but beneath the surface was as unpleasant as the Spy Master himself, Joseph Fouché.

How could the Earl not realise when she looked at him with her seductive eyes that she was evil?

She might be interested in him as a man, but she was prepared to murder those he had commanded, and only so that she could wear a white ermine stole.

"I hate her! I hate her!" Shenda said over and over again as she helped Lady Gratton into a gown of *diamanté*-spangled gauze which had obviously cost an astronomical sum.

"How many have died to provide her with that?" she asked herself.

She had finished arranging Lady Gratton's hair and clasped round her neck a diamond necklace. Then, looking at her reflection in the mirror, Her Ladyship said:

"The other women staying here will want to scratch my eyes out to-night! How can His Lordship notice any of them when he can look at me?"

She was speaking almost to herself.

As Shenda heard her words and the hard satisfaction in her tone, she felt a sudden constriction of her breast.

Bad, wicked, criminal she might be, but she was very beautiful!

As she thought of the Earl kissing Lady Gratton, she remembered the sensations that his lips could arouse.

It was then, as she felt as if there were a sharp dagger stabbing her in the heart, that she knew that she loved him.

* * *

The following morning the whole Castle was a-flutter, as everybody, including His Lordship, was to depart for London immediately after an early luncheon.

There was a mountain of trunks to be carried downstairs to travel in the brake drawn by six horses.

They would also take with them the lady's-maids and the valets of the visiting guests.

By some clever contrivance on Mrs. Davison's part, Shenda was not to travel with the other servants, but instead was to go to London in a travelling chariot with Mrs. Davison herself.

"I have to purchase," she had said firmly, "some new linen for the Castle, and I've no intention of allowing anyone to choose it but myself, knowing where her late Ladyship always shopped, and where she obtained the very best linen."

She smiled as she spoke, and Shenda said:

"Thank you, thank you! I know you are doing this for me."

"I am looking forward to the trip," Mrs. Davison answered firmly, "and I know if his Lordship asks questions, when I explain, he'll agree I've done the right thing."

It flashed through Shenda's mind that the Earl might have thought of something like that himself.

Then she told herself he thought of her as only a seamstress.

He would think perhaps she liked the company of the rest of the staff, who were laughing and giggling amongst themselves as they climbed into the brake.

They took only a little over two hours to reach London from the Castle.

The Earl's fastest horses were employed and were drawing the lightest vehicles.

Lady Gratton had left earlier, driving with the Earl in his Phaeton drawn by his team of perfectly matched chestnuts.

With a little pain in her heart Shenda watched them leave.

Lady Gratton was looking very beautiful, her high-crowned bonnet trimmed with small ostrich feathers.

When she had been dressed and ready to leave her bedroom she had turned to Shenda and said:

"I have enjoyed my visit to the Castle, and I know it will be the first of many. Do not forget to bring the gowns I want altering."

"I'll do my best, M'Lady," Shenda said quietly.

"There are a lot to be done in London, and as you realise, I must look my best to please such a fastidious gentleman as His Lordship."

She looked in the mirror and said as if speaking to herself:

"He is a very, very attractive man!"

Shenda clenched her fingers together until the knuckles went white.

"What has he . . . said? What has he . . . done to make Lady Gratton . . . speak like that?" she asked herself.

Was he acting the part she knew he would have to do, or was he really in love?

Then she was ashamed of herself for doubting his loyalty to England.

And yet as she watched them drive away she thought that no two people could appear more perfectly matched when it came to looks.

Perry Crawshore was following them in another Phaeton, and the rest of the gentlemen were accommodated in coaches and carriages, some their own and others which belonged to the Castle.

The Earl, as he drove away, was not thinking of his guests or of Lucille, sitting beside him.

He was thinking of what he would say to Lord Barham and how last night he had been suspicious of the young Baronet who worked in the Admiralty.

Because he was a friend of Perry's, it had not really struck the Earl that he was in the Admiralty until he remembered Lord Barham had said that information was coming, incredible though it seemed, from his own office.

The Earl had therefore contrived to talk to Sir David Jackson alone.

"Are you enjoying work with Lord Barham?" he asked. "I have always admired him tremendously."

"I have hardly seen him since he took over from Lord Melville," Sir David replied.

"Then you do not work for him directly," the Earl said.

"No, I work with the Second Secretary," Sir David replied. "It seems strange, but he is a Frenchman!"

The Earl was instantly alert, but he did not show it.

"A Frenchman?" he repeated, his voice drawling a little as if he were not particularly interested.

"Oh, you need not be suspicious of him," Sir David said. "*Comte* Jacques de Beauvais is the son of an *émigré* who was one of Louis Fifteenth's most important and aristocratic Ambassadors."

"Really!" the Earl exclaimed.

"He came to England," Sir David continued, "at the very beginning of the Revolution and was brought up here. He went to School at Eton."

The Earl laughed.

"That certainly sounds very reliable!"

"He has a fanatical hatred of Napoleon," Sir David went on, "because his grandmother, although she was very old, was guillotined, and the family *Château* was not only pillaged, but also set on fire."

"He certainly has no reason, then, to like the French!" the Earl remarked.

"No, indeed," Sir David replied. "He raises his glass to Napoleon's downfall at every meal, and buys us all a drink when the news comes through a French ship has been sunk."

He looked at the Earl admiringly as he said:

"We had quite an orgy in the office when the news came through that you had personally sunk two of France's best first rates at Toulon!"

"I was very fortunate," the Earl said. "The wind changed at exactly the right moment, or I might not be here now!"

"What I want to do," Sir David said, "is to get back to my Regiment. My leg is much better, but the Doctors will not give me a clean bill of health for another six months or so!"

"Well, I am sure, in the meantime, you are doing a good job," the Earl said.

At the same time, he had a feeling he would like to know a little more about the *Comte* Jacques de Beauvais.

He might be as whole-heartedly in favour of winning the war as Sir David said.

However, one never knew for sure, and for the moment he felt, after the treachery of Lucille, he could trust no-one.

Then he told himself he must not become obsessed with hounding out spies to the point where he did not think clearly, and became fanatical on the subject.

He had known men like that in the past and always thought them slightly unbalanced.

He drove, keeping his horses at a sharp pace.

Despite the cooing voice of Lucille Gratton paying him compliments and sitting a little nearer to him than was necessary, he was thinking of Shenda.

He was wondering if he had made a terrible mistake in allowing her to go to London.

chapter six

THE carriage dropped Mrs. Davison at Arrow House in Berkeley Square.

Shenda thought the house was very impressive, as it had a lantern on brass supports fixed to the railings, which were tipped with gold.

She longed to look inside, but Mrs. Davison, having alighted, told the coachman to take her to Lady Gratton's house.

This, Shenda found, was in one of the streets which connected with Berkeley Square and was a small residence set between two much larger ones.

It was attractively furnished, and she discovered that there was a large Dining-Room and a small Sitting-Room on the Ground Floor.

On the First Floor there was a big Drawing-Room, and above that there was Lady Gratton's bedroom, which looked out onto the back of the house so that it was quiet.

Shenda expected that she would have to sleep in the attic.

It was a relief to learn there were only three bed-rooms, which were occupied by two maid-servants and the lady's-maid, who was still in bed with a fractured leg.

She was, therefore, told that for the moment she must use a small bedroom which was opposite to Her Ladyship's.

It adjoined a Dressing-Room which was used by Sir Henry when he was at home.

Shenda's room was very small, and a huge wardrobe containing Her Ladyship's clothes covered one wall.

When she entered it, she saw the bed which stood in one corner was covered with at least a dozen of Her Ladyship's bonnets.

One of the maids helped her to move these into boxes which they placed on top of the wardrobe, but even then there was hardly room for Shenda to turn round.

But at least, she thought, she had a room to her-self.

She had been half-afraid that she would be ex-pected to share one either with the lady's-maid who was indisposed, or else with one of the housemaids.

She was unpacking Lady Gratton's trunks and hanging up her gowns in the wardrobe when Her La-dyship arrived.

She was looking exceedingly beautiful, but when she came nearer Shenda felt herself shudder.

"As soon as you have finished unpacking," she said in an authoritative tone, "I will show you the gowns that I wish altered, and as quickly as possible!"

Shenda felt inclined to reply that she would find it difficult to work in such a small place.

Then she suddenly became aware that if she were to find out anything important, it might be useful to be so near to Her Ladyship's bedroom.

She therefore finished emptying the trunk, which was taken away by a man-servant, and went to her own room to await Her Ladyship's orders.

When she could see the pile of alterations that Lady Gratton gave her, it was not difficult to tell the maids that, as she had so much work to do, she would eat in her own room.

She knew they would resent having to carry a tray upstairs.

At the same time, she was aware that unlike those at the Castle, the servants were not the best type and obviously had no liking for their mistress.

As she might have expected, her supper, when it arrived, was cold and not very appetising.

She told herself that she must expect to make sacrifices if she was to help the Earl.

As she thought of him while she was eating, it was easy not to notice what she was putting into her mouth.

'I must help him . . . I must!' she thought.

When Lady Gratton came up to bed Shenda forced herself to be pleasant while she helped her mistress undress.

There had been two elderly gentlemen to dinner who, she learnt, were relatives who had just returned to London.

They did not seem to be of any particular consequence as far as she was concerned.

She gave them only a cursory glance over the banisters as after dinner they moved slowly up the stairs and into the Drawing-Room.

Shenda was, in fact, feeling very tired by the time Lady Gratton came up to bed.

It had been a long day.

Also, because she was nervous about what she was doing, she felt as if the walls of the small house were pressing in on her like prison bars and that she might find it difficult to escape.

She thought she was being over-imaginative, and it was a relief to hold Rufus in her arms and know how much he loved her.

She had taken him for a walk down the street while Lady Gratton was having dinner.

She longed to turn into Berkeley Square and look again at Arrow House.

Then she decided that if by some mischance the Earl should see her, he would either think she was being curious about him, or else neglecting her duties.

Now, as she caressed Rufus, she said in a whisper:

"I hope we shall not be here too long. I know you want to be back at the Castle . . . and so . . . do I!"

She found herself thinking how handsome the Earl had looked yesterday when he had stood waiting for her in the Greek Temple.

It struck her that he might almost be a god himself, perhaps Apollo, bringing light to all who sought it.

Then she remembered how he had kissed her and knew it would never happen again.

When he had no further use for her, it would be all that she would have to remember.

"If I were sensible, I would leave the Castle and the village and go somewhere else," she told herself.

But she knew the only place she had to go to was her uncle's house.

Therefore, she would cling to her position as Seamstress until it was completely untenable.

When she had finished helping Lady Gratton to undress, she thought Her Ladyship would get into bed.

She was wearing one of her transparent night-gowns, but to Shenda's surprise she said:

"Fetch me my thicker *négligé*. It is hanging in my wardrobe and it is made of blue satin and trimmed with lace."

Shenda fetched it, and as Lady Gratton put it on, she saw it was an expensive and a very beautiful garment.

It was so lovely that she wondered why Her Ladyship wanted it at this moment, when she was alone with no-one to see her.

Her thoughts were interrupted when Lady Gratton said:

"You can go to bed now, as I shall not need you again. Call me at ten o'clock as usual, and I hope you will be up early so that you can start on the alterations I have given you. Then we can fit the gowns later in the morning."

"I will do that, M'Lady," Shenda replied.

She glanced around the bedroom to ensure that it

was tidy, then went out of the room, closing the door behind her.

Rufus was waiting for her in her small bedroom and jumped up eagerly when she appeared.

She put him on the bed while she undressed, slipping into the pretty nightgown which her mother had made for her.

She put over it a robe of fine wool which had no ornamentation except for some pearl buttons and a narrow row of lace round the small collar.

It was a robe she had worn for several years and made her look very young.

But it was warm and comfortable, and she wanted to read for a little while before she went to sleep.

She had just sat on top of the bed and arranged a candle in the right position so that she could see clearly what she was reading, when she heard Lady Gratton's bedroom door open.

She wondered if Her Ladyship was coming to ask her for something, in which case she was sure she would disapprove of Rufus being on her bed.

She moved forward to pick him up and put him on the floor when she heard Lady Gratton pass her door and move down the stairs.

"I wonder what she wants?" she questioned.

It seemed strange that Her Ladyship, who never did anything for herself, did not call for her to fetch whatever it was she required.

Then she told herself that she should be grateful that she was free for the moment from being given orders and having to obey a woman she hated and despised.

She knew both her father and mother would have

been very shocked at the thought of her being involved with anyone so despicable, or, for that matter, acting the part of a servant, and even coming to London to do so.

She thought, however, that her father would understand her reasons for wishing to help the defeat of Napolean, who at the moment had almost the whole of Europe under his heel.

It seemed terrifying to think that such a tyrant, a man whose cruelty had shocked and horrified the whole of England, should have only the British Navy between him and complete victory.

"Please . . . God . . . let us . . . win!" Shenda prayed.

As she did so she heard the sound of a carriage stopping outside the house.

Because this seemed strange at so late an hour, she jumped off the bed and, going to the window, carefully pulled back the curtains.

Below she could see the top of a closed carriage with a coachman on the box and a footman who was opening the door.

Then she was aware that a man was alighting and thought perhaps it was Sir Henry Gratton returning unexpectedly.

It was then she remembered that Lady Gratton had just gone downstairs.

In which case, although she was in her night attire, she was perhaps expecting the man who had just arrived.

Moving from the window and letting the curtain fall back into place, Shenda blew out the candle by her bed.

She put on the soft velvet slippers which matched her dressing-gown and very, very quietly turned the handle of her door.

Her heart was beating uncomfortably because she was so frightened.

As she peeped out she saw Lady Gratton's door was ajar, which meant she had not returned to her room.

Moving very slowly to the top of the staircase, and keeping back against the wall so that she could not be seen from below, Shenda listened.

It was then she heard a rat-tat on the front-door, so faint that it would not be heard by the man-servant who slept in the basement.

Then she was aware that somebody, and she knew it was Lady Gratton, was moving from the Drawing-Room down the stairs and into the hall.

There was the sound of a key being turned in the lock, and a flash of light as the door opened; there were footsteps and she heard it close again.

Then in a low voice Lady Gratton said:

"I thought you had forgotten me!"

"You must forgive me, *Ma Chérie*," a man replied, "there was a sudden crisis at the Admiralty, and it was impossible for me to get away until now."

"You are here, and that is all that matters!" Lady Gratton said. "Come up to the Drawing-Room."

Shenda heard them walk up the stairs and go into the Drawing-Room.

As they shut the door she knew she had to hear what they were saying.

The man had spoken good English, but she had not missed the French endearment, and she was quite

123

certain that this was the man the Earl was trying to identify.

Moving slowly and completely silently on the thick carpet, she reached the Drawing-Room door and stood still outside it.

It was not of heavy mahogany like those in the Castle, and she could hear Lady Gratton laugh before she said, obviously in answer to a question from her Caller:

"Yes, it was a most enjoyable party, and as I told you, the Earl is completely infatuated with me!"

"Then keep him that way!" the man said in a deep voice.

"Help yourself to a glass of champagne," Lady Gratton suggested, "then we can talk."

"But first I must tell you how alluring you look, and how utterly and completely desirable! I have missed you, *Ma Petite*!"

For a moment there was silence, and Shenda had the idea that the Caller was kising Lady Gratton, and holding her close against him.

Then he said, and his voice seemed a little deeper:

"I need a drink! *Mon Dieu*, they say that Frenchmen can talk, but so do Admirals and politicians, and it is difficult to stop them!"

Lady Gratton laughed.

Shenda was aware that the Caller had walked across the room to where there must be a table containing drinks.

There was the clink of glasses, then the sound of footsteps as he re-crossed the room to hand Lady Gratton a glass.

"A toast, *Ma Chérie*, to your beautiful eyes, your

irresistible lips, and your exquisite and very desirable body!"

Lady Gratton laughed.

"As usual, Jacques, you are very poetical."

"How could I be anything else with you?" he replied.

At last Shenda felt that they were sipping their champagne.

Then, in a voice that sounded as if he were impatient, the man Lady Gratton had called Jacques said:

"What news have you for me? And speak in French. It is safer!"

Again Lady Gratton laughed.

"You are quite safe here, and you know you always tease me about my accent!"

"Only because I love your broken French as I love everything else about you!" he replied. "Now, what news have you for me?"

There was a pause before Lady Gratton said in rather bad French and with a very obvious English accent:

"The Earl is not certain, but I gather he thinks the Secret Expedition is bound for the West Indies."

Jacques made a sound of satisfaction.

"That is exactly what Bonaparte thinks, and he will be delighted to know that his assumption is, as usual, correct!"

Jacques drew in a deep breath before he continued:

"I heard from one of my friends two days ago that the Emperor plans to scare Downing Street into dispersing its slender Military Forces. Now he will know that he has succeeded!"

It struck Shenda that Jacques was talking almost to himself rather than to the woman with him.

Then Lady Gratton said softly:

"I am glad you are pleased, Jacques."

"I am delighted!" Jacques replied.

"And I will . . . get . . . my reward?"

There was a note of greed in her voice which was over-eager.

"But of course," Jacques replied, "and knowing that you have never failed me, I have brought what I promised you with me."

"Five hundred pounds?" she asked excitedly.

"It is here."

There was a pause, then a slight sound as if Jacques were bringing something out of his pocket.

"Oh, Jacques, how wonderful!" Lady Gratton exclaimed. "It is just what I wanted to buy myself something very, very special! Thank you, you are such a kind and good friend to me."

She was speaking in English, but Jacques replied in French as he asked:

"And what about Nelson?"

Again there was a pause before Lady Gratton answered:

"Alas, I could get no sense out of His Lordship with regard to the Admiral. Quite frankly, I think he does not know."

"You do not think he suspects that you have any reason for asking such questions?"

Now there was a hard, frightening note in the Frenchman's voice.

"No, no, of course not!" Lady Gratton replied quickly. "Why should he suspect for one moment that I have any ulterior motive in asking what our most famous sailor is doing?"

"I suppose everybody talks about him," Jacques said reflectively.

"Of course they do, but personally, I find that all heroes are boring, especially when they are away for so long that I cannot even remember what they look like!"

Jacques laughed.

"Nevertheless, you must try again," he said. "It is very important for the French to know exactly where the man is. He has caused us enough trouble already by turning up where he is least expected!"

"I will try to find out," Lady Gratton promised, "and I do try, Jacques, to do what you want."

"I shall have some more questions of importance by the end of the week," Jacques replied, "and any information you obtain will be amply rewarded."

"You are so generous," Lady Gratton gushed.

As Shenda listened, there was a little sound beside her.

She was suddenly aware that Rufus had followed her from the bedroom and the noise he had made was almost like a sneeze; perhaps the dust had tickled his nose.

Before she could move, or realise what was happening, the door of the Drawing-Room was wrenched open and a man confronted her.

"Who are you? What are you doing here?" he asked, and in the darkness his voice seemed to ring out terrifyingly.

For a second everything was swept from Shenda's

mind except that the man facing her seemed menacing.

She knew that if he was convinced she was spying on him, he might even attack her physically.

It was as if her heart had stopped beating, and it was impossible to breathe.

Then it flashed through her mind that if he accused her of being a spy, he might also suspect the Earl.

It was then, as if her father were guiding her, that she knew what to reply.

"I . . . I am sorry if I . . . disturbed you, Sir," she said in a childlike voice, the words coming jerkily from between her lips, "but . . . my little dog asked . . . to go out . . . and I am taking him into the . . . street."

For one terrifying second she thought the Frenchman did not believe her, and as if to look at the dog he moved a step forward.

Then, as he saw Rufus beside Shenda, he paused, and as he did so Lady Gratton said from behind him:

"It is all right. It is only my lady's-maid."

Feeling as if she were moving in a nightmare, Shenda bobbed a little curtsy and, holding on to the banisters, moved on down the stairs.

She had gone a few steps before she was aware that Jacques had moved back into the Drawing-Room.

As he did so he said in French, and in a low voice:

"Il faut la tuer!"

Her hand was on the lock of the front-door before she realised what he had said:

"She must be eliminated!"

It was almost as if the sentence were in front of her in letters of fire.

For a moment she felt as if she could not move because of the horror of it.

Then, as she opened the door, Rufus went out and she followed him.

The servants on the box of the carriage waiting outside the house stared at her in surprise as she walked past.

Then, almost as if she were being directed, she moved slowly and unhurriedly, forcing herself not to give in to the panic that was sweeping over her.

" *'Il faut la tuer!'* "

It was what she might have expected, she thought, from one of Bonaparte's spies, who would take no chances that he himself might be discovered.

It seemed as if it took her an hour to walk to the corner of the road and into Berkeley Square, but somehow she got there.

Then, when she was out of sight of the carriage, she started to run, moving faster than she had ever moved in the whole of her life.

She tore up the side of the Square to where the Earl's house was situated, and when she reached it saw the lantern was still alight in front of the door-way.

Suddenly she remembered with horror that she might have been followed, and the footman on the carriage would know where she had gone.

She looked back and, to her relief, as she could see quite clearly in the moonlight, there was no-one to be seen.

She ran up the steps and, raising the knocker on

the front-door, moved it up and down, not noisily, just in case the sound should carry in the quiet of the night.

She was afraid it would alert the coachmen, or the man who was with Lady Gratton.

It seemed a century of time before the door opened.

Then the night-footman peered out, his eyes a little bleary, as if he had been asleep in the padded chair provided for him in the hall.

Shenda looked at him and saw to her relief that it was a boy from the Castle whom she had known for years.

"Is . . . His Lordship . . . at home . . . James?" she asked breathlessly.

She moved as she spoke through the open door to stand beside him.

"Ow, it's you, Miss Shenda!" he said in surprise. "'Is Lordship's in there!"

He jerked with his thumb towards a door at the other end of the hall.

"Oi'll tell 'im you're 'ere," he said, "after Oi've shut t'door."

But Shenda did not wait.

She ran across the hall, opened the door into what she was to learn later was the Earl's Study, and entered.

He was standing at the window which opened onto a small garden at the back of the house.

He turned round in surprise.

Because Shenda was so frightened, and because she could think of nothing but that he must save her,

130

she flew across the floor and flung herself against him.

"I . . . I have f-found your spy!" she gasped. "And . . . he . . . he is . . . going to . . . kill me!"

The words were almost incoherent, but nothing seemed important except that the Earl was there and that he would save her!

She hid her face against his shoulder.

As his arms went round her, he could feel her whole body trembling against him.

"It is all right," he said quietly. "He shall not harm you."

"H-he . . . s-said," Shenda whispered, "'*il faut . . . la . . . tuer!*'"

She could hardly say the words.

Yet she knew she must impress on him the danger she was in from the relentlessness of Napoleon's spies.

"He . . . may kill . . . you . . . too . . ." she whispered.

Then, because everything was so terrifying, and because she was afraid not only for herself, but also for the Earl, she burst into tears.

The Earl held her closer.

As he did so he knew what he had felt for Shenda was what he had never felt before for any other woman.

He wanted to protect her; he wanted to take care of her.

Most of all, he wanted to keep her from coming in contact with anything so unpleasant as the perfidy of Lucille, the cruelty of Napoleon's underlings, and the

Social World of London, where innocence and purity had no place.

Then, as Shenda went on crying helplessly against him, he knew he had fallen wildly and irrevocably in love.

* * *

Lucille Gratton poured herself another glass of champagne.

She was aware as she did so that her visitor was standing just inside the Drawing-Room door with a scowl on his face.

"Stop worrying, Jacques," she said. "I brought the girl here from the country because she is a Seamstress. She is young and stupid, and I am sure harmless."

"You told me there was nobody in the house to overhear us!" Jacques said accusingly.

"How was I to know that the stupid little wretch would take her dog out at this time of the night?" Lady Gratton asked.

"She is dangerous!" Jacques said. "I will send some tablets over to-morrow morning, and you must see they are put in her food or what she drinks."

"You really mean to kill her?"

"She will be eliminated, which is a better word!"

"Oh, really, Jacques," Lady Gratton protested, "I cannot have dead bodies lying all over my house! You know perfectly well if anyone knew of it they would talk. And besides, she has come from the Castle."

"Even people who come from Castles can die!" Jacques retorted sarcastically. "And it will be an excuse for you to sympathise with the Earl, and make him realise how sorry you are that he has lost one of his servants."

"Oh, really!" Lady Gratton said petulantly. "How can I concern myself with servants when you are with me?"

She set down her glass of champagne and put her arms around his neck.

"Dearest Jacques," she said, "I like you best when you are making love to me."

For a moment he resisted her and did not respond, then he asked in a different tone:

"Is that what you want?"

"How can I not want it where you are concerned?"

She raised her lips to his and as he kissed her she was aware that she excited him.

"Let us go upstairs," she said. "That tiresome girl will have returned by now."

Jacques was re-filling his glass of champagne as Lady Gratton went to the door.

Looking down, she saw that the front-door was still open.

"She is not back," she said in a whisper, "and that makes things even easier. Come upstairs and shut the door behind you."

Jacques did as he was told.

However, he paused for a moment to look at the open front-door just below him.

"Jacques!"

His name, spoken in a low voice, had a longing and a passion which he found irresistible.

Swiftly because he was nervous, he hurried up the next flight of stairs and into her bedroom.

The Earl had taken Shenda to a sofa beside the fire-place and fetched her a glass from the grog tray.

She shook her head when he offered it to her, and he said gently:

"Drink a little. It will do you good."

Although he had diluted the brandy, she felt it moving fierily down her throat and gave an involuntary shudder.

At the same time, the feeling of faintness and sense of collapse which had made her cry seemed to evaporate.

She tried to wipe away her tears with the back of her hand, and he gave her his handkerchief.

It made her think of how he had bandaged Rufus's paw in the wood.

For the first time since she had rushed headlong through Berkeley Square to Arrow House, she looked down nervously to see if Rufus was with her.

He was curled up at her feet and she gave a little cry of relief.

"Rufus . . . saved . . . me!" she said to the Earl.

He put his arm round her shoulders.

"Now, tell me everything that happened from the very beginning."

She wiped away the last of her tears, saying as she did so:

"I . . . I am . . . sorry."

"There is nothing to be sorry about," he replied. "You have been so unbelievably brave, but for the moment we have to be sensible and decide what must be done. Tell me what you heard."

Hesitatingly, but at the same time acutely aware that the Earl's arm was round her, she told him exactly what had happened since she arrived at Lady Gratton's house.

When she got to the part where Lady Gratton told Jacques what she had learnt about the Secret Expedition, she hesitated.

A look of anxiety filled her eyes as if she could go no further.

"Tell me what she said," the Earl said gently.

"She said . . . you had told her . . . that the . . . Secret Expedition . . . had . . . gone to the . . . East and . . . West Indies."

She had turned her face away as she spoke, but now she looked up at him and said frantically:

"Y-you . . . could not . . . you did not . . . betray them?"

"Do you really think I would?" he asked.

"N-no . . . but that . . . was what . . . she said . . . but . . . but how . . . could she have . . . known?"

"What she said was a lie!" the Earl said quietly.

"You are . . . certain?"

"Perfectly certain, and I can tell you now it was in fact exactly what the Admiralty wanted Napoleon Bonaparte to think."

Shenda drew a breath of sheer relief.

"Could you believe," the Earl asked, "that I would be so foolish, especially after you had warned me, to tell Lady Gratton anything that might jeopardise our ships and those who sail in them?"

Because what he said sounded accusing, Shenda hid her face against his shoulder.

"Forgive . . . me," she whispered. "I . . . I knew

135

you would not . . . do such a thing willingly . . . but I thought . . . perhaps she had . . . used some psychic power . . . or perhaps a . . . drug to make you talk in your sleep."

"She did none of those things," the Earl said. "Now, tell me the rest of the story."

Because she was so relieved, Shenda told what had happened next, quickly and without hesitation.

Only when she spoke the sentence in French which she had overheard as she reached the door and knew was her death-knell did her voice tremble.

Then in a little more than a whisper, she said brokenly:

"I . . . I do not . . . want to . . . d-die!"

"It is something which will not happen," the Earl said, "at least not for many, many years!"

"Y-you will . . . save me?"

"Would you expect me to do anything else," he asked, "when you have been so marvellous, so utterly and completely wonderful?"

"Do you . . . know who . . . the spy is?"

"I know who he is, and it will be he and not you, my darling, who will die!"

Shenda looked up at him as he spoke.

He felt her body stiffen against him, and her eyes widen so that they seemed to fill her whole face.

"Wh-what . . . did you . . . s-say?" she asked in a voice he could hardly hear.

"I called you 'my darling,'" the Earl replied, "which is something you have been for a long time, although I fought against it. I love you, Shenda, and I want to know what you feel about me."

Shenda lifted her face, and his lips came down on hers.

He kissed her as he had once before, but in a very different way.

Now his kiss was demanding, possessive, as if he wanted her and yet was afraid he might lose her.

To Shenda it was as if the Heavens had opened and the stars had fallen down into her heart.

His lips aroused in her a sensation she had felt once before when he had kissed her by the wood, but now because she loved him it was a million times stronger and more wonderful.

She knew then that as he kissed her and went on kissing her, she gave him not only her heart, but also her soul.

Only when he raised his head did she say incoherently, but with a rapture the Earl had never heard before in any woman's voice:

"I love you...I...love you! But...how can you...l-love me?"

"Very easily," the Earl replied, "and I promise you, my precious, nothing like this will ever happen to you again. Never will I involve you in anything that is so frightening, or so dangerous!"

"But...I wanted to...help you."

"I know you did, and it was unbelievably brave, but now you have to be sensible enough to realise that I must act quickly, so that that tool of Napoleon shall not escape."

Shenda thought for a moment.

Then, as if she forced herself to think of what had happened rather than the wonder of the Earl's lips, she said:

"When I . . . left the house . . . I did not shut the door . . . and they will . . . know that I have . . . not returned."

For a moment the Earl's arms held her closer still, as if he were protecting her.

Then he rose to his feet, and as she saw the expression on his face she knew he was a man going into action.

"I will take you upstairs," he said, "so that you can go to bed. You will be safe because I shall tell my valet who was with me when I was at sea to look after you, and protect you."

"You are . . . leaving me?" Shenda asked in a low voice.

"I am going to Lord Barham to tell him that you have solved his problems. He will take over and—"

He paused.

"In the meantime," he said as if he were speaking to himself, "that devil may get away!"

There was something in the way he spoke which made Shenda feel afraid.

"W-what are you . . . going to d-do?" she asked.

The Earl did not reply.

He walked out of the room and into the hall to where the footman was sitting in his padded chair.

As the Earl appeared, the footman jumped to his feet.

"Wake every man in the house," the Earl ordered. "Tell them to dress immediately. Hurry, there is no time to be lost!"

It was the word of command from a man who was used to giving them.

James ran quickly down the passage which led to

the Pantry and the rooms beyond it, where the men-servants slept.

While he was speaking, Shenda had come from the Study to stand beside him.

He took her hand and they went up the stairs together and along the passage into what she guessed even before they entered it was the Master Bedroom.

It was an impressive room, but not so large or so grand as the one occupied by the Earl at the Castle.

Here there was a small, thin, wiry-looking man whom Shenda thought she would have known if she had seen him anywhere as being a sailor.

He jumped to his feet as the Earl entered.

"Hawkins," the Earl said, "Miss Shenda is in danger. She is to sleep in my bed until I return. Get your pistol and shoot anybody who attempts to enter the room and disturb her—do you understand?"

"I understands, M'Lord!" Hawkins replied.

The Earl turned to Shenda.

"I promise you will be safe."

"And . . . you will . . . take care of . . . yourself?"

She was suddenly desperately afraid for him.

He smiled at her, then, before she could say any more, he was gone and she could hear him running down the passage and back to the hall.

She was sure by this time that most of the men in the house had assembled and were waiting for him.

Because she wanted to run after him, because she felt suddenly lost and lonely and not certain what she should do, she just stood in the Earl's bedroom.

She looked at the big, canopied bed with its heavy curtains and the coat-of-arms of the Earls of Arrow embroidered over the headboard.

"Now, Miss, you get into bed," Hawkins said, "and don't worry. 'Is Lordship know 'ow to look after hisself, as he's looked after us all, ever since we've bin wiv 'im."

"Supposing . . . supposing the . . . Frenchman . . . shoots him?" Shenda said in a very small voice.

Hawkins smiled.

"You can bet yer last penny that 'Is Lordship will shoot 'im first! Now, come on, Miss, orders is orders, an' 'Is Lordship expects 'em to be obeyed!"

Shenda laughed a little, as if she could not help it.

She did not even feel embarrassed as Hawkins pulled back the sheet and helped her into bed.

He was just like her Nanny used to be.

"Now then, in case you're worried," he said, "Oi'll be sittin' just outside yer door, me pistol in me 'and, an' if anyone comes nosing around, they'll get a piece o' lead right through the 'eart! I'm a good shot, I am, even if I says it meself, though I shouldn't!"

Shenda tried to smile.

"Thank you . . . and I am . . . sure I shall be . . . quite safe."

Hawkins blew out the candles and walked towards the door.

"Goo'-night, Miss, an' God grant us a fair wind t'-morrer!"

It was something she guessed he must have often said to the Earl when they were at sea.

Then, as she shut her eyes she thought of his arms around her, as once again he was kissing her, and his lips were on hers.

"I love him . . . I love him!" she whispered.

Then she knew that if only he loved her in return, then all her dreams had come true.

But she was half-afraid that she was only dreaming.

chapter seven

THE Earl, with his small private Army of retainers, came back to Berkeley Square in triumph.

The dawn had broken and already the streets were filling up with people starting work.

The Earl was driving his own closed carriage.

As he drew his horses to a stand-still, the carriage door opened and the men of the household got out.

Although they had been up all night, their cheeks were flushed and their eyes were shining.

The Earl knew as he walked into the house that the night was something they would remember all their lives.

When he had left Shenda in the care of his valet, he had gone downstairs to the hall.

As the men-servants came hurrying as they had been told to do, they looked at him apprehensively.

In a quiet, clear voice he told them why he wanted them.

He knew that just as happened on board ship when he asked for volunteers, there was not a man among them who would not be prepared to do anything he demanded.

He sent the youngest footman to wake the coachmen and tell them to bring his closed carriage by a different route to Lady Gratton's house.

Then he and the six men that were left set off down the Square, but not efore three of them he could trust as well as he himself were armed.

As he had hoped, the men in charge of the *Comte*'s carriage were half-asleep on the box.

They took very little notice of three men walking on one side on the road, two on the other and two more a little way behind them.

Only as the Earl and Carter walked in through the open front-door of the house did the coachman look up in surprise.

At the same moment, he was pulled from his seat on the box.

As the Earl disappeared inside the house the same thing was happening on the other side of the carriage to the footman.

The Earl walked very softly up the stairs, finding it useful that he knew his way in the house, although he did not like to think why he had been there before.

Carter followed him.

He was over fifty, but looked young for his age, and he had been a footman at the Castle before he had gained his position as Butler at Arrow House.

The Earl reached the main bedroom and paused

for a moment outside the door so that Carter could join him.

Then the two men walked in, their pistols in their hands, and Lady Gratton gave a shrill scream of horror.

The Earl permitted the *Comte* to dress himself, and when he had done so, told Lucille to do the same.

By this time she was sobbing and pleading with him, but he had not even looked at her.

Only when the *Comte*, his face dark with fury and fear, was ready, did the Earl say sharply:

"I will allow Your Ladyship to dress alone, but there is no escape from this room, except through the door. My assistant will be waiting outside it to make sure you do not attempt to do anything foolish."

"Where are you taking me? What are you doing? How can you behave in such a cruel way to me, of all people?" Lucille screamed.

The Earl did not deign to answer.

He merely forced the *Comte* to walk in front of him, and with a pistol pointing at his back took him down the stairs.

At the bottom two footmen were waiting, and on the Earl's instructions they tied the *Comte*'s arms behind him and put a rope which they had brought with them round his legs.

The Earl then looked outside the front-door to see if his carriage had arrived as he had ordered and saw to his satisfaction that it had.

His coachman and footman were on the box, their faces alight with curiosity.

Knowing the *Comte* would undoubtedly try to

bribe his servants if he was left alone with them, the Earl told one of his men to gag him.

He made it clear he wanted it done in such a way that it would be impossible for the Frenchman to speak.

On the Earl's instructions they put him on the back seat of the carriage, and when they had done so, he told one of his men who was armed to sit opposite him, and shoot him if he tried to escape.

Then he went back into the house to find that Lucille, who was still crying, was coming down the stairs.

She started to plead with him, but he stopped her by raising his hand for silence, and saying in a hard voice:

"I am afraid, My Lady, your wrists must be tied to prevent you from trying to help your confederate to escape."

"He is not my confederate," Lucille screamed, "he forced himself upon me, and I could not refuse to do what he wished. I hate the French! I know they are our enemies, but he was strong and I was weak!"

The Earl did not bother to answer.

He only watched to make sure her wrists were tied together, so that she could not use her hands.

Then he told his men to assist her into the coach.

It was then he had the coachman and the footman who had been driving the *Comte*'s carriage put inside it with two men to guard them.

He told his own servants to drive that coach, while he would drive his own.

They were obviously astonished, but did as he said, and he drove off.

Carter was beside him while the rest of his men crammed onto the box of the carriage containing the *Comte*'s drivers.

The streets were empty, but there was the moonlight to guide their way to the Tower of London in what the Earl thought was record time.

When he arrived there he sent for the Lieutenant-Governor of the Tower.

Brought from his bed, he was an elderly man who had been in his time an excellent General. He listened attentively to what the Earl had to say and replied:

"I know that Lord Barham, who is an old friend of mine, will be extremely grateful to Your Lordship. Bonaparte's spies are, I believe, everywhere, and the sooner this one is executed after due trial, the better!"

"That is what I thought myself," the Earl said.

The Lieutenant-Governor hesitated.

"What about Lady Gratton?"

"I think, as an example to other women not to emulate her," the Earl replied, "after due trial she should be kept in custody until the end of the war."

"I agree with you!" the Lieutenant-Governor exclaimed. "And in spite of the behaviour of the French, an Englishman still dislikes killing a woman!"

"I think in this case it would be in actual fact more merciful than knowing she will be ostracised by Society for the rest of her life!" the Earl remarked.

Then, because he found it hard to talk of Lucille, he said quickly:

"I have brought two other men, a coachman and a

footman, who have been driving the *Comte*."

"Do you think it likely they are involved in any way in his nefarious activities?" the Lieutenant-Governor asked.

"Most unlikely," the Earl replied, "but they will know which people he has called on, and the women with whom he is constantly in contact. If we are lucky, we will learn the addresses of other spies in London, like himself, and better still, those who carry the information he obtains to France."

The Lieutenant-Governor nodded.

"You are undoubtedly right, My Lord," he said, "and they will both be interrogated as quickly as possible, and before those who are involved with the *Comte* have any idea that he is missing."

The two men shook hands and soldiers took the *Comte* in one direction and Lucille Gratton in another.

The Earl ordered his coachman to back the *Comte*'s carriage into the court-yard.

He told his men to get into his and drove away.

By this time, the stars had faded and the first light of dawn was creeping up the sky.

The Earl drove to Admiralty House.

The sentries looked at the carriage in surprise, but did not prevent Carter from stepping down from the box and approaching the front-door.

There were two footmen on duty and, when the Earl asked to see Lord Barham, an Officer who was obviously in charge appeared first.

A few sharp sentences from the Earl sent him hurrying upstairs to wake the First Lord.

The Earl waited only a few minutes in a room

downstairs before Lord Barham joined him.

He was wearing a long robe over his nightshirt, but he looked alert and despite his age had the same buoyancy about him he had always had on the quarter deck.

"Is it good news or bad, Arrow?" he asked as he came into the room. "I know it must be something sensational to bring you here at this hour."

The Earl paused for a moment, as if to make his announcement even more dramatic.

"I have just, My Lord," he said, "taken your First Secretary the *Comte* Jacques de Beauvais to the Tower of London!"

*   *   *

Because he wanted to get back to Shenda, the Earl did not linger at the Admiralty.

He merely gave Lord Barham a brief account of exactly what had occurred, then, having promised to return later in the morning, drove his horses to Berkeley Square.

When he and his servants had entered the house and followed him into the hall, he said:

"We have to-night struck a blow against the Emperor of France, but as unfortunately there are other spies in our midst, I am ordering you to tell no-one of what has happened. Also, say as little about it as possible, even amongst yourselves!"

He thought the men looked disappointed, and he added quietly:

"You have excelled yourselves, and done exactly what I expected, but if we are to do the same thing again in the future, it would be a mistake if our prey, who I can tell you is more wily than any reptile, escapes before we have a chance of catching him."

He saw by the men's faces that they understood, and he went on:

"I trust you to keep your mouths shut, your ears open, and your eyes keen for the sake of England."

There was an expression on their faces that told him better than if they had cheered that they would all do what he asked.

Then he hurried up the stairs.

As he expected, he found Hawkins sitting alert with a pistol in his hand outside the bedroom door.

He did not speak, but merely smiled at the man and opened the door very quietly.

By the daylight coming through the sides of the curtains he could see that Shenda was asleep

She looked small and insubstantial in the great bed, and with her hair falling over the pillows, very young and innocent.

The Earl stood looking at her for some minutes, then he moved quietly out of the room and closed the door.

* * *

Shenda woke slowly, feeling as if she had slept for a long time.

Then she thought of the Earl and was suddenly alert.

She sat up in bed, knowing as she did so that she was in the Master Suite, and that the Earl had gone away to tackle the *Comte*.

If he had not returned, perhaps the *Comte* had

struck first, and the Earl might be injured or even killed!

Because the idea was so horrifying, involuntarily she gave a little cry, and as she did so, the door opened.

Hawkins put his head inside the room and asked:

"Are you awake, Miss Shenda? It's time for your breakfast."

"Is . . . His Lordship . . . back . . . or is there . . . any news of h-him?" Shenda asked breathlessly.

Hawkins came into the room.

"'E's back, 'appy as a sandboy at havin' won a great victory, an' despite what 'e tells me, I'm letting 'im sleep."

Because she was so relieved, Shenda felt the tears prick her eyes, then in case Hawkins should see them, she looked at the clock on the mantelpiece.

"What . . . time is . . . it?"

"It's nearly ten, Miss, an' 'Is Lordship didn't get in 'til after seven."

"What could he have been doing all that time?" Shenda asked.

"I 'spect 'Is Lordship'll want to tell you that 'is-self, Miss," Hawkins replied. "I'll fetch your breakfast."

He disappeared, and Shenda sank back against the pillows.

The Earl was safe!

Whatever else had happened, the *Comte* had not harmed him, and as long as she remained here, she too was safe.

"I love him!" she whispered. "But . . . although he . . . said he loved me . . . perhaps it was just . . .

because last night I was . . . so upset . . . and he wanted to . . . comfort me."

At the same time, as Shenda was trying to calm the excitement rising within her, she knew that her heart was singing.

* * *

The Earl awoke, realised he was not in his own bed, and remembered what had happened.

He had told Hawkins to call him at eight-thirty, but he could see by the clock on the mantelpiece that it was after ten.

He told himself the man had no right to disobey his orders.

But he knew however much he might remonstrate with Hawkins, he would insist on doing what he thought was best for his well-being.

He got out of bed, pulled the bell violently, and when Hawkins appeared he was carrying a tray on which there was his breakfast.

"I told you to call me at eight-thirty," the Earl said.

"There now!" Hawkins exclaimed. "I thinks I must 'ave made a mistake. Wot with keepin' meself awake on duty, so to speak, while Your Lordship was gaddin' about th' town, I must 'ave misunderstood wot Your Lordship says to me!"

As he finished speaking he put the tray down on a table in the window, and as he did so a footman appeared with a number of other dishes.

This prevented the Earl from saying any more, but as he shrugged himself into his robe he asked:

"Is Miss Shenda all right?"

"I've jus' taken in 'er breakfast, M'Lord," Hawkins replied. "Worried, she was, about Your Lordship. I reassured th' young lady by sayin' you was 'ome, safe an' sound!"

He went from the room as he finished speaking, and the Earl gave up the hopeless task of trying to reprimand him.

Having eaten a hearty breakfast, by the time he had taken a bath and dressed he learnt from Hawkins that Shenda had been shown to a room where she could dress.

She had expected there would be nothing for her to wear but the nightgown and woollen robe she had worn when she had run in fear and terror from Lady Gratton's house to find the Earl.

When she entered her bedroom it was to find Mrs. Davison waiting for her, and her own trunk half-unpacked.

"Now, what have you been up to, Miss Shenda?" Mrs. Davison asked. "When I hears that you'd arrived last night, I thought you might have asked for me!"

"You are here now, and that is all that matters," Shenda said evasively, "but how were you so clever as to get my trunk?"

"It's only just arrived, Miss Shenda," Mrs. Davison said, "and 't'was Mr. Carter who sent for it, seeing as how without it you'd've had nothing to wear!"

Shenda knew that Mrs. Davison was dying with curiosity.

She somehow managed to evade giving her any positive answers to her questions, knowing she must wait to hear what the Earl would say first.

She was so eager to see him that it was difficult to understand what Mrs. Davison was saying.

When she was ready, wearing the pretty gown she had made herself, she hurried down the stairs.

She was still afraid that what had happened last night was just an illusion.

Perhaps to-day she would face a different reality.

*　　*　　*

In a way the Earl was thinking very much the same thing.

He knew that last night when Shenda had come to him trembling with fear that he had forgotten everything but her loveliness, the softness of her body, and the unusual sensations she evoked in him.

Now, in the harshness of day, he knew he had to face the question as to whether it was possible for him to marry her, considering she was in fact only one of his servants.

Since he had inherited the title, it had been impossible not to realise that as the Earl of Arrow he had a great and responsible position.

The whole family looked to him as their leader and guide in the same way as the men he commanded at sea had done.

To do anything that would lower the reputation of a family as important as the Bows was unthinkable.

Of course, Shenda appeared to be a Lady in every sense of the word.

He had never met anyone so sensitive or who responded so naturally to what he might call the behaviour and instinct of being "gentleborn."

But in that case, why was she working as a Seamstress?

If she was an orphan, she should be with her relatives, and certainly chaperoned by some older woman.

Yet every nerve in his body told him how much he wanted her.

The love he had acknowledged to himself last night swept over him like a tidal wave.

He knew he had never in his whole life felt for any woman what he felt for Shenda.

He would kill any man who insulted her, and yet that was exactly what he would do if he could not offer her marriage.

"Oh, God, what am I to do about her?" he asked as he finished dressing.

As he walked down the stairs he was vividly conscious of the portraits of his ancestors looking down at him from their gold frames.

He thought the men of the Bow family would understand what he felt; it was the women who would not only disapprove, but denounce the marriage as being a *mésalliance*.

He was aware how easily they could make Shenda's life a living Hell if they treated her as a servant who had pressured her Master into matrimony.

He crossed the hall knowing he would find Shenda in the Study, where she had come to him last night.

He asked himself again what he could do about what appeared to be an impossible situation.

Then, as he opened the door and saw her standing

at the window, the sun turning her hair into a halo, he felt his heart turn a dozen somersaults.

He knew that without Shenda he had no wish to go on living.

He shut the door behind him and just held out his arms.

She gave a little cry that was like the song of the birds and ran towards him.

"You . . . are . . . safe! You are . . . safe!" she murmured.

"I am safe, and so are you," the Earl said in his deep voice.

Then he was kissing her and the whole world stood still.

He kissed her fiercely, as if he were afraid she might vanish.

As he felt his heart respond to the wonder of it, he knew it was what Shenda was feeling too, and her eyes, when he looked into them, were dazzling.

Her whole face was transfigured with a beauty that was, the Earl knew at the back of his mind, not human, but Divine.

"I love you!" he said. "My darling, I love you!"

"H-he did not . . . hurt you?"

"No, he did not hurt me."

He had no intention of telling Shenda that he had found the *Comte* in bed with Lucille.

He thought it would shock her and he himself did not want to remember the degradation of what had occurred.

"I . . . prayed and . . . prayed that you would be . . . all right," she was saying in her soft voice, "and then . . . and I cannot think how it . . . happened . . . I . . . fell asleep!"

"You were very tired, my precious, after all you had been through," the Earl said.

He looked down at her, then as if he could not help himself, as if his lips said the words for him, he asked:

"How soon will you marry me, for I know, Shenda, that I cannot live without you."

"D-do you . . . really . . . want me?"

"More than I can tell you in words," the Earl answered.

Then he was kissing her possessively, demandingly, as if he would never let her go.

*   *   *

Centuries later, or at least that is what it seemed, the Earl drew Shenda to the window and they looked out at the flowers in the garden.

"We will go back to the Castle to-morrow," he said, and his voice sounded strange even to himself. "We will be married in the chapel by the new Vicar who, I understand, is moving in to-day."

"How I wish . . . Papa were . . . alive," Shenda said softly. "I know how . . . proud he would have been . . . to perform the . . . Service."

"Your father was a Parson?" the Earl asked.

He spoke a little absent-mindedly, because he was still thinking how difficult his relations might be when they knew whom he had married.

It also flashed through his mind that perhaps he was making a mistake, and because Shenda had worked at the Castle he should marry her in London, where she was unknown.

Shenda stared at him, then she said:

"Have you . . . really asked me to . . . marry you . . . without knowing . . . who I . . . am?"

The Earl pulled her a little closer to him.

"It does not matter to me who you are," he said, "or where you come from. I know only that you are mine, Shenda, and that I want you as I have never wanted a woman or anything else in my life before!"

"When you . . . speak like that," Shenda said, "I . . . I want to . . . cry. It is how I . . . always wanted to be . . . loved . . . as Papa loved . . . Mama. But I was afraid it was . . . something that would . . . never happen."

"When I kissed you in the wood," the Earl said, "I thought you were not human but a nymph, a sprite from the magic pool, or perhaps a little goddess who had assumed human form."

He moved his lips over the softness of her cheek before he went on:

"Since then I have thought of you, Shenda, dreamt of you, and kissed you, but it never seemed important to know your other name."

She gave a little laugh.

"No-one will ever believe that, but let me tell you now that my name is Lynd, and Papa was the Vicar of Arrowhead for seventeen years!"

The Earl stared at her.

"If that is true, why were you working in the Castle?"

"I was . . . hiding."

"Hiding? From whom?"

"From having nowhere to go when your Agent, Mr. Marlow, said he wanted the Vicarage for the new incumbent."

"But—how is it that you had nowhere to go?" the Earl asked, feeling stupid because he did not understand.

"I . . . I have no . . . money," Shenda said simply, "and . . . when I talked to Mrs. Davison . . . she let me come to the . . . Castle thinking I . . . I would be . . . safe with her . . . and the new Earl would . . . never find out that . . . I was not a . . . proper servant."

"My darling, thank God you came to the Castle!" the Earl said, "and that I found you in your magic wood!"

"How could I have . . . known or guessed that you were the . . . Earl that nobody had . . . seen? But . . . when you kissed me . . . I thought it was . . . something I would . . . never forget."

She gave a little laugh:

"No-one would . . . believe this has all . . . happened . . . because I was . . . kissed by a stranger."

"A stranger who fell in love," the Earl said as he smiled, "and it will be an exciting story to tell our children."

Shenda blushed and hid her face against him.

He thought her shyness so adorable he kissed her until they were both breathless.

Then, as he raised his head, the Earl said:

"We are already one person, my darling, and I have the feeling that no Service can make us belong to each other more than we do already."

"How can you . . . say anything so . . . wonderful?" Shenda asked. "And it is what I . . . feel myself . . . I am yours . . . as I have really been ever since you . . . kissed me."

"No-one could be more brave or done more than you have," the Earl said.

She knew he was speaking of what had just happened, and as he felt her shiver he said:

"Forget it, and if I have to do anything in the future to help England, you will not be involved."

Shenda gave a little laugh, and it was a very happy sound.

"I think . . . if I am your . . . wife . . . it would be very difficult for you to . . . do anything unless I knew about it . . . and how could I not . . . help you and . . . want to be . . . with you?"

The Earl pulled her against him.

"I love you!" he said. "But what I have to do now is to see Lord Barham, and as soon as that is settled, if he does not keep me too late, we will leave for the Castle."

"And . . . shall we really be . . . married to-morrow?" Shenda asked.

"I suppose, in order to do so, I shall have to get a Special Licence," the Earl said.

"I think . . . if we are both residents . . . in the same Parish . . . it is . . . unnecessary," Shenda said hesitatingly, "but you could . . . ask the Parson to . . . make sure."

"I expect somebody at the Admiralty will be able to tell me," the Earl replied. "It would be embarrassing to have to confess that I do not even know the name of my own Vicar!"

Shenda laughed.

"As long as you remember my name and my old last one, that will be all right."

"You told me it was Lynd," the Earl said.

"Shenda Lynd, and Papa used to hunt with the pack of fox-hounds your father the late Earl supported when he was well enough to do so. In fact he was known as the 'Hunting Parson'!"

"I seem to remember people speaking about him when I was a child," the Earl remarked.

Then he looked at Shenda and asked:

"I still cannot understand why, when you were turned out of the Vicarage, you had nowhere to go. You must have relatives somewhere?"

"My uncle lives in a house in Gloucestershire where Papa was brought up," she explained, "and although he is Lord Lyndon he is . . . very poor and has a . . . large family. I thought therefore that he would not want anybody . . . extra in the house . . . and of course . . . with Rufus, that made . . . two."

She was smiling, then realised the Earl was looking at her somewhat strangely.

"Are you telling me that your uncle, and of course your grandfather before him, was Lord Lyndon?" he asked.

"Yes!" Shenda replied. "And for that matter, Papa was an 'Honourable.' But it did not make us have any more money after Mama died and the small allowance she received from her mother was stopped."

Her voice dropped as she said:

"Mama's father was a Scotsman—the Laird of Kintare and he was . . . furious with Mama for . . . marrying . . . a Sassennach!"

"It sounds very Scottish to me." The Earl smiled.

Then, as if she were a child, Shenda hid her face against his shoulder as she said:

"I had to sell . . . all the furniture we . . . owned in . . . the Vicarage to pay the . . . debts we owed to the . . . tradesmen and when I came to . . . the Castle, I had only a few pounds left . . . which is all I . . . have now!"

The Earl did not miss the note of anxiety in her voice, as if she were afraid he would be shocked at her being so poor.

His lips were against her forehead as he said:

"My darling, you shall never be poor again. There is so much I want to give you, so much I want to share with you."

What he said came from his heart.

At the same time, he said silently a prayer of gratitude.

It did not matter to him who Shenda's family was, but that she was the niece of Lord Lyndon and her grandfather was a Scottish Laird would certainly receive the approval of his relations.

They could not scorn her and there was no reason for them ever to know that she had played the part of a Seamstress at the Castle.

He understood now why Mrs. Davison had been so perturbed when he told her Shenda was to act as lady's-maid to Lady Gratton.

"How could I have been so obtuse?" he asked himself. "Why did I not make enquiries about her and find out exactly who she was?"

Then he knew that it did not matter.

She was everything he wanted—the woman who belonged to him, the woman who was the other half of himself.

She was also an ethereal, spiritual being who had lifted his eyes to the stars and could make him believe he could touch them.

Her beauty was like the Castle, and their children, and please God he would have a number of them, would carry on the traditions of his family.

They would dedicate their lives to the service of England, and it was difficult for him not to be overwhelmed by the wonder of it.

He held Shenda even closer than she was already, and his lips were on hers.

As he kissed her he dedicated himself both to his country and to her.

He knew that together they could bring happiness and understanding to so many people.

"I love you!" he said.

Now his voice seemed almost to ring out in the quietness of the room.

"As . . . I love . . . you!" Shenda said. "I am so . . . happy . . . so unbelievably happy! I feel that Papa and Mama have . . . looked after me . . . and helped me to . . . find you."

"I think actually I found you!" the Earl said. "And it is not only the most intelligent thing I have ever done in my life, but also the most wonderful!"

He looked down at her for a long moment before he asked:

"How can you be so perfect? How can everything about you be exactly what I wanted and was quite sure I would never find?"

"Please . . . go on thinking that," Shenda said, "and I pray that God will make me . . . exactly what you want . . . and that you will go on loving me . . . for the rest of our lives."

"You may be quite certain of that," the Earl said, "and now, my darling, I must leave you, otherwise I shall undoubtedly be reprimanded by the First Lord!"

Shenda laughed.

"That is something that must certainly not happen!"

"I cannot bear to leave you," the Earl said. "You must take care of yourself until I return."

"I . . . will do that," Shenda answered, "but . . . there is . . . something I want to ask you."

"What is it?"

"Do you think . . . if we are to be married . . . that I could buy . . . just one or . . . two gowns so that I can . . . look pretty in them for you?"

The Earl laughed.

"How could I possibly have forgotten that a bride, even if she is enveloped in the magic of the woods and the light from the stars, still wants a wedding-gown?"

To Shenda's surprise he walked away from her and tugged on the bell-pull.

She stood looking at him in wonder until a few seconds later the door opened and Carter asked:

"You rang, M'Lord?"

"I want my Phaeton immediately," the Earl said, "and ask Mrs. Davison to come here. Three grooms are to be ready to deliver messages in Bond Street."

If Carter was surprised, he was too well-trained to show it.

"Very good, M'Lord," he said respectfully, and went out, shutting the door behind him.

Shenda ran towards the Earl.

"What is . . . happening? What are you . . . doing?" she asked.

"I am sending for the best Dressmakers in Bond Street to come here immediately," the Earl replied. "You and Mrs. Davison will decide what is wanted. Choose yourself what is needed for to-morrow and perhaps the next two days, and the rest can follow as soon as they are ready."

Shenda gave a little gasp.

"And, darling," he added, "I am a very rich man, so I want my bride, who will be the most beautiful Countess of Arrow there has ever been, at least to rival the Queen of Sheba!"

Shenda laughed. Then she said:

"I do not . . . believe this . . . is true! I know I am . . . dreaming."

"Of course you are," the Earl replied, "and I am going to make absolutely certain that we never wake up!"

As if he could not help himself, he kissed her again, passionately, demandingly, and fiercely.

At the same time, she was aware she excited him, and it gave her a wonderful, warm feeling that she could do so.

There was something in his kisses that was like the magic she had first found in the woods.

There was something she knew in her prayers, and that was that her father and mother were near her.

It was all part of the love which filled her heart, and which she knew now was in the Earl's heart too.

It was the love that was Divine and which came

from God, who had protected her and brought her and the Earl together.

It was love which would remain with them, not only in this world, but in the world to come, and for all eternity.

ABOUT THE AUTHOR

Barbara Cartland, the world's most famous romantic novelist, who is also an historian, playwright, lecturer, political speaker and television personality, has now written over 495 books and sold nearly 500 million copies all over the world.

She has also had many historical works published and has written four autobiographies as well as the biographies of her mother and that of her brother, Ronald Cartland, who was the first Member of Parliament to be killed in the last war. This book has a preface by Sir Winston Churchill and has just been republished with an introduction by Sir Arthur Bryant.

Love at the Helm, a novel written with the help and inspiration of the late Earl Mountbatten of Burma, Great Uncle of His Royal Highness The Prince of Wales, is being sold for the Mountbatten Memorial Trust.

She has broken the world record for the last thirteen years by writing an average of twenty-three books a year. In the *Guinness Book of Records* she is listed as the world's top-selling author.

Miss Cartland in 1978 sang an Album of Love Songs with the Royal Philharmonic Orchestra.

In private life Barbara Cartland, who is a Dame of the Order of St. John of Jerusalem, Chairman of the St. John Council in Hertfordshire and Deputy President of the St. John Ambulance Brigade, has fought for better conditions and salaries for Midwives and Nurses.

She championed the cause for the Elderly in 1956 invoking a Government Enquiry into the "Housing Conditions of Old People."

In 1962 she had the Law of England changed so that Local Authorities had to provide camps for their own Gypsies. This has meant that since then thousands and thousands of Gypsy children have been able to go to School, which they had never been able to do in the past, as their caravans were moved every twenty-four hours by the Police.

There are now fourteen camps in Hertfordshire and Barbara Cartland has her own Romany Gypsy Camp called Barbaraville by the Gypsies.

Her designs "Decorating with Love" are being sold all over the U.S.A. and the National Home Fashions League made her, in 1981, "Woman of Achievement."

She is unique in that she was one and two in the Dalton list of Best Sellers, and one week had four books in the top twenty.

Barbara Cartland's book *Getting Older, Growing Younger* has been published in Great Britain and the U.S.A. and her fifth cookery book, *The Romance of Food*, is now being used by the House of Commons.

In 1984 she received at Kennedy Airport America's Bishop Wright Air Industry Award for her contribution to the development of aviation. In 1931 she and two R.A.F. Officers thought of, and carried, the first aeroplane-towed glider air-mail.

During the War she was Chief Lady Welfare Officer in Bedfordshire looking after 20,000 Service men and women. She thought of having a pool of Wedding Dresses at the War Office so a Service Bride could hire a gown for the day.

She bought 1,000 gowns without coupons for the A.T.S., the W.A.A.F.'s and the W.R.E.N.S. In 1945 Barbara Cartland received the Certificate of Merit from Eastern Command.

In 1964 Barbara Cartland founded the National Association for Health of which she is the President, as a front for all the Health Stores and for any product made as alternative medicine.

This is now a £300,000 turnover a year, with one third going in export.

In January 1988 she received "La Médaille de Vermeil de la Ville de Paris." This is the highest award to be given in France by the City of Paris for achievement—25 million books sold in France.

In March 1988 Barbara Cartland was asked by the Indian Government to open their Health Resort outside Delhi. This is almost the largest Health Resort in the world.

Barbara Cartland was received with great enthusiasm by her fans, who fêted her at a reception in the City and she received the gift of an embossed plate from the Government.